"*Reply All* is a thrilling collection: laugh-out-loud funny and
achingl
undern
And or
brillian
the zeit
served
Reply A

—ROBE
A Good

"In this
continu
incapab
less tha
no hum
behavio
mercur
and cur
their ma
irresisti
worldly

—MELI
Disappe

break away books

reply all

stories

robin hemley

INDIANA UNIVERSITY PRESS   BLOOMINGTON & INDIANAPOLIS

This book is a publication of

Indiana University Press
601 North Morton Street
Bloomington, Indiana 47404-3797 USA

iupress.indiana.edu

Telephone orders 800-842-6796
Fax orders 812-855-7931

∞ The paper used in this publication
meets the minimum requirements of
the American National Standard for
Information Sciences—Permanence
of Paper for Printed Library Materials,
ANSI Z39.48–1992.

*Manufactured in the United States
of America*

Library of Congress Cataloging-in-
Publication Data

Hemley, Robin
Reply all: stories / Robin Hemley.
    p. cm.
  ISBN 978-0-253-00180-1 (pbk. : alk.
paper) — ISBN 978-0-253-00186-3 (ebook)
  I. Title.
  PS3558.E47915R47
2012
  813'.54—dc23

                    2012005741

1 2 3 4 5 17 16 15 14 13 12

For Barry Silesky & Sharon Solwitz,
with great affection and
admiration.

The heart deceives, because it is never anything but the
expression of the mind's miscalculations...
I don't know what the heart is, not I:
I only use the word to denote the mind's frailties.

MARQUIS DE SADE

contents

acknowledgments

I'd like to express my gratitude to a number of friends, mentors, and colleagues who have helped me with these stories and to the editors who first published these stories: Barry Silesky, Sharon Solwitz, Bret Lott, David Shields, Dinty Moore, Michael Martone, Barry Hannah, Elizabeth Stuckey-French, Gerald Shapiro, Robert Olen Butler, Patricia Foster, Heather Bryant, Robert Stewart, Philip Graham, Kathleen Anderson, and Linda Oblack.

"Reply All" appeared first in *Another Chicago Magazine* (ACM) and was later reprinted in *New Sudden Fiction* (Norton) and *Writing Fiction;* "Local Time" first appeared in the *Southern Review;* "The Warehouse of Saints" first appeared in *9th Letter* and was reprinted in *Best American Fantasy;* "Magellan Stew" first appeared in *Another Chicago Magazine;* "The 19th Jew" first appeared in the *Chicago Tribune* and won first place in the Nelson Algren Award for Short Fiction competition and was later reprinted in *Jewish American Fiction: A Century of Stories;* "Devotion" first appeared in *20 Over 40;* "The List" first appeared in *Tribe;* "Redemption" first appeared in *Another Chicago Magazine.* "The Underwater Town" first appeared in *Shenandoah.* "St. Charles Place" first appeared in *Hobart.* "Dead Silence" first appeared in *New Letters.*

reply all

The Warehouse of Saints

Too many blessings break a man apart.
—TOMAZ SALAMUN

Today, we did inventory, my son Domenic and I: ten shinbones belonging to St. Timothy. Sixteen tibias of Paul. Four skulls of John the Baptist. Three complete skeletons of Mary Magdalene. A jar of teeth simply labeled "Assorted Saints." A cask of desiccated organs. Thirteen livers of St. Peter. The dried tongues of Judas Iscariot, Simon, and Thomas. Fingernail shavings of the great kings of France, including the entire big toenail of Richard the Lionheart. His entrails, too. The scapulas of Saints Catherine and Michael. Enough True Cross splinters to build a bridge from Chinon to Paris. God even sends us bones on His day of rest, and that confounds me. Are all other mortals deemed worthy enough to share in His rest, except us, His bone slaves?

"Does it concern you, my son, that Saint Peter had so many livers, and Mary Magdalene so many skeletons within her?" I have asked him this question and variations upon it before, but my son is clever, and I marvel at the many reasons we should revere God's contradictions. If God did not prefer the impossible to the possible, and the incomprehensible to the comprehensible, he would not have bothered to give form to the firmament and breath to the earth's confounding creatures. Domenic has reminded me of the loaves and fishes, of the water into wine, of the Holy Trinity, of Christ's body and blood.

"The Jews believe that ten thousand people heard Moses at Mt. Sinai," he says, combing his beard with a comb carved from the ribs of St. Batholeme. "Every Jew alive today has a piece of one of those souls co-mingled with his own. What the Jews believe is not what I believe, but I use this as an example. The sums of God are not our sums."

I am a simple man. Such faith inspires me—though there are times, I admit, that I doubt the good Domenic and I do. I named my son after Saint Domenic, who appeared to me in a dream and cut off his index finger and gave it to me. He said, "Mathias, even the whitened bones of the saints clamor to do God's bidding." Yet, it took sixteen years before the true nature of Domenic's prophecy was revealed to me. In the early years, I sold herbs and potions concocted by my wife. Only after her death, when our future looked bleakest, did the bones and relics start to mysteriously appear at the mouth of our cave. Then I understood my true calling. In the two years since, Domenic and I have built our business into the largest inventory of bones and relics of saints in the Loire Valley.

Domenic bows his head and tells me that if the Lord's ways were not mysterious, they would not be the Lord's ways and there would be nothing He could do to inspire or impress us. Man should not try to explain everything in the world and beyond. Still, I wonder. That is my sin. Wonder. And from wonder sometimes doubt springs.

Our tufa stone cave is narrow but deep. Only six cows could fit side by side at its entrance, but a herd could be driven in and disappear within its belly. I have not explored its depths. I stay near the entrance, where the light from the sun mingles with the candles we have placed within the niches and shelves we have carved into the soft stone. Domenic is a tall boy and although the ceiling is higher than his head, he often bends as though in reverence.

We live in a murderous region, my son and I, a place never to my knowledge visited by angels and saints. In Chinon, the Dauphin reigns in his Chateau, though not unthreatened. His own mother would betray him to the English and says he is a bastard. In such a world, is it a surprise then that more travelers are murdered on the road to Chinon than make it through alive? Bandits are our true rulers, and the Dauphin, under whose protection we live, can stop neither a brigand from slitting my throat, nor a witch from making a changeling out of me, nor the English from making a mockery of the French monarchy. In my youth, things were much better. You could walk the streets of Chinon at night, no one locked his door, and everyone greeted his neighbor.

Even in our cave, we hear the rumors, and many believe that France is doomed, that before long an English king will rule over us all. A week ago, the Dauphin was visited by a girl who calls herself Jehanne from the village of Domrémy, who said she was heaven-sent to lead him to victory against the English. She speaks for God, the people say, and they brought her to see the Dauphin, but the Dauphin's advisors, fearing she might have been sent by the English to murder him, put an impostor on the throne. When she was led to the throne room, the impostor said, "I am the heir to the kingdom of France," but this girl ignored him and pointed to the Dauphin, hiding in the crowd. She knelt before him and said, "Gentle Dauphin, I have come, by the grace of the King of Heaven, to raise an army and see you crowned in Rheims." That she was not beset upon by bandits in the Forest of Chinon on her way to meet the Dauphin had already convinced many that she was under God's protection, but what she said to the Dauphin, in front of scores of witnesses, has made even him willing to listen. I am not so sure I would call the Dauphin gentle. In Asay le Rideau, a few of the Burgundian guard once insulted the Dauphin and so he set the town ablaze and put to death hundreds of their number. Still, I prefer the Dauphin I know to the Dauphin I don't, and we must forgive him his occasional outbursts.

This Jehanne, if she speaks for the King of Heaven, is not the first woman in this place to have God's ear. In Fontevraud, it has been decreed that the head of the order will always be a woman—in this way, the men who serve under her learn humility. The present Abbess, Blanche D'Harcourt, is generous with the humility she doles out to the monks. Men at the Abbey eat no meat, only fish, and receive a daily ration of a quarter liter of wine to the nun's half a liter. If not for the problem of the wine ration, I could be a monk at Fontevraud. I have no difficulty bending to the will of a woman. My own Genevieve spoke regularly with

God, though He never told her anything grand to do. God gave her the ingredients to use when mixing her tonics and potions and taught her the language of chickens and wild boars. Useful yes, from time to time, but nothing that inspires reverence and awe. Still, she was able to foretell her own death when she overheard the chickens speaking of it one gray morning as she approached the henhouse.

Today, I have found a neat stack of bleached bones by the entrance to the caves. They do not always arrive so. They appear in the mornings, arriving from where I do not know. Heaven-sent, Domenic says. Sometimes they arrive in sacks, sometimes moldered, sometimes with bits of sinew and clumps of hair and clothing attached, sometimes the individual bones, the smaller ones, are wrapped in sausage casings. Through divination, we come to understand to which saint the bones belong. Domenic is good at this. I have never been so good at divination, except for my dream of Domenic's finger.

Domenic and I often laugh about the first time I pulled a skull from one of these sacks and ran into the fields, staying until nightfall. "Father," Domenic called, "this is the head of John the Baptist. We are saved!"

"We are doomed," I called from among the wheat fields. "Where did this skull come from? It smells of earth and worms. We'll be hanged, drawn apart, and then, Mother of Mercy, excommunicated. You must bury it again—the crossroads of Fontevraud and Couziers would be a good place. At midnight. And you must blindfold the skull so it will not find its way back to us. Then you must go to mass, have neither food nor drink, cease urination for four days, and spit whenever you hear the words 'owl,' 'vagina,' or 'potato.' You must never speak to anyone of this." The words "owl," "vagina," and "potato" had formed unbidden in my mind, but why these words, I can't say. I only know that "owl," "vagina." and "potato" made me feel great foreboding and so I thought maybe this was a sign from God. And spitting never hurts.

"Father, it's the dream. Your dream," Domenic shouted. "We are saved, not doomed. We must tell everyone." Now we keep this head, our first Saint, up in the front of the cave, by the money box in a special niche, for good luck.

"Good news, Father," he tells me now, appearing out of the dark, where I do not like to go. "We can fill the order from the Abbess in Fontevraud."

"An order from the Abbess?" I say, staring at a group of pilgrims making their way toward us from the river Vienne. "I don't remember such an order."

"It was only a week ago," he says. "A large quantity of pelvis."

"Another miracle," I say, bowing my head in prayer.

We can hardly keep the pulverized pelvis of the Holy Virgin in stock—it's been out of stock for months. A spoonful mixed into the mortar of a church before consecration, chapel, abbey, or cathedral (proportions vary, depending on altitude) will ensure entry into heaven for all the congregants and their livestock—when mixed with the tepid breast milk of the mother of a stillborn boy infant with eleven toes, it is said to cure gout and taste delicious, but this I cannot verify.

"Domenic," I say, "God's mercy is great, is it not?" I meant to say this in praise, but my tone of voice was not the one I intended. I sound doubtful. I have dreams and visions I cannot understand. Angels with swords slitting the throats of Cathar children. Poisonous flowers fluttering from heaven. Last night, I dreamed of a field of dead popes, each of whom was disinterred to receive communion. One pope lay in his casket, blind, while a priest teased him with a communion wafer. Then the pope's tongue burst into flame. Why am I tormented with such undecipherable visions?

Domenic kneels beside me. He rarely answers a question without giving it great thought first. He swats some flies from my nose and lips. I crane my neck around him to note the progress of the pilgrims. Soldiers walk among them. Although I can't recognize any faces, the sun glints off the soldier's armor. One carries a staff bearing a strange seal.

"Father," he says. "Have you been thinking of the Albigensians again?"

"The wretched Albigensians," I say.

"The Albigensians were heretics," he says. "It is God who grants mercy, the devil who shuns it. If you pity the Albigensians so, why did you name me after the saint who wiped them from the earth?"

Domenic does not understand. It's not so much pity that plagues me as a nagging thought. I can't give voice to the thought, so heretical is it, and for this reason it keeps rising. Perhaps these thoughts were planted in me by the devil. I know I would be burned at the stake if I told anyone of them besides Domenic. I think these thoughts, I believe, because I'm surrounded by the bones of the saints, and they talk to me. They whisper doubt to me, not faith. What if the Albigensians were right? What if man is evil, as I've heard the Albigensians believed, and the only way to redeem himself is to suffer multiple lifetimes? What if Pope Innocent and Saint Domenic did an evil thing in hounding and slaughtering the Albigensians by the thousands, and in so doing, eradicated our chance to redeem ourselves through their teachings? I'll never know, but maybe we're on the wrong path, not the right one. Is it possible Saint Domenic proved the Albigensians right by killing them?

Domenic stands and plucks a hair from his beard, examines it, and lets it fall to the dirt. He turns slowly as the wind carries the shouts of the group toward us.

At the head of the group of soldiers and townspeople rides a stout boy on a mare. The boy carries a white banner I've never seen: against a field of lilies are written the words "Jhesus Maria," and underneath these words is a picture of Christ surrounded by two angels. The boy wears a black cap, boots, leggings, and a tunic that reaches to his knees. A coat of arms, red and gold, blazes from the tunic. We have had important visitors before, princes and bishops and cardinals, all drawn to this place to see what we have to offer. Some send their emissaries, but most choose to visit in person. Buying the bones of a saint is a delicate business—the buyer wants to know what he's getting, wants to see it, wants to heft its holy weight and hear it whisper its secrets and tell one's destiny if it wishes. One cannot send an emissary for that. But this banner the boy carries is such I've never heard of nor seen, and I feel a peculiar tingling in my toes, an ache as though my own bones were struggling to answer some invisible summons and rise bidden from my body.

A voice somewhere inside me speaks. "Jehanne," it calls. "Jehanne." I turn to alert my son, but he has already retreated into the cave. "Domenic, come out," I say. "You must see this."

"I saw it," he answers, his voice suddenly sulky.

"But I think it's that woman we keep hearing about, dressed like a man," I say.

"That's right," he says. "I have an intimation." The boy is always having intimations, often accompanied by a headache. And he starts to pray the special prayer to ward off women who dress like men.

"But Domenic. She carries a banner with our Lord's name on it."

He doesn't pause his prayer but only prays louder. Presently, the voices of the crowd gather at the mouth of the cave and one voice, surprisingly deep for a girl so young, sounds above the rest.

"Troglodytes!" the woman hails us. "I wish to speak with you about the relics you trade in. We ride to Orleans soon to break the siege of the English."

The girl dismounts her horse. In the air, a faint whiff of honeysuckle wafts, the swish of her horse's tail, the nonsensical song of Jerome, the town imbecile, always lagging last in any procession.

"We're closed for inventory," Domenic shouts. "Don't touch anything." But they seem not to hear him. As if in a dream, they have already started milling about the shelves, picking up relics. Domenic stands among them, grabbing the relics from their hands and replacing them in the niches. Two men and one woman lie prostrate before the three skeletons of Mary Magdalene.

"Holy!" one murmurs.

"Preserve us," another says.

"What's this?" Jehanne asks, picking up the lucky skull of John the Baptist.

"That's John the Baptist," I tell her. "Very rare. Our first saint."

"Look, it's the toe of St. Ignatius," a monk from Fontevraud shouts to his brother.

"Put it back," the brother says. "What are we going to do with the toe of St. Ignatius?"

"What *can't* be done with the toe of St. Ignatius?" the first monk says. "Never was there such a versatile saint! Not only was he the child the Savior took up in his arms as described in Mark 9:35, but he was among the auditors of the apostle St. John and the third Bishop of Antioch, if we include St. Peter."

"Oh, there you go again," says the second monk. "The third Bishop of Antioch, *if* we include St. Peter."

"Oh, luckless bones, I hear your voices," Jehanne says. "This is nothing but the daughter of a farmer from Bourgueil."

The anguish of her voice cloaks me like another skin and I look at my hands as though they hold my answer to her. But they do not. They are dumb and cannot speak. No part of me can speak with the certainty of this Jehanne. They cannot even speak the terror of my doubt.

I bring her a stool to sit on and walk to the well to give her something to drink. "No, it's John the Baptist all right," I say, my voice betraying me. "But he's not for sale."

"Where did you get these?" she says, sitting down with John's skull and looking into his sockets.

"Here and there," I say. "Domenic, do you want to tell her? It's really quite an amusing story! That very skull you're holding was our first relic, wasn't it, Domenic?" I laugh and turn to Domenic, who seems to be quaking. He stares at the girl. And I stop to stare at him. An excuse for him begins to form: the dankness of the cave has made him shiver. But I cannot say this and believe it. This is my own son. How can I doubt my son? Even if he is wrong, I would wish anything but doubt. I wish his certainty again.

"Bourgueil?" he asks her in the slightest voice I've ever heard from him.

Jehanne casts the skull in the dirt and produces a piece of worn leather from her robe. She holds the leather kerchief in front of Domenic. As she unwraps it, we strain to see what the leather holds, a bone small and curved like a rib, but brittle, covered by a thin red dust.

"Domenic," she says. "Tell me from whose body this was taken?"

Domenic stops shaking and peers at the bone, then carefully plucks it from its wrapping. She's so much smaller than him. She's a girl who looks like a boy and wears men's clothing. Maybe she's a witch. He looks into his hand as though he has never seen a bone before.

"More light," he says. "I need light," and one of Jehanne's followers, a boy wearing a tunic with Jehanne's crest crudely stitched onto the cloth, takes a torch from the wall of the cave and brings it to Domenic.

He touches his beard and closes his eyes. He makes the sign of the cross and we all cross ourselves, even Jehanne, who looks at him otherwise without emotion. He puts the bone to his nose and sniffs it, then breathes its scent deeply. He places it by his ear and listens to the voice of the bone. He places the bone to his brow and divines the thoughts of the bone, or its teachings if it belongs to a saint. He nods and nods again and the light of the cave trembles because the boy holding the torch has begun to shiver.

"This is a splinter from the ribs of the Savior Himself," he announces in his normal ringing voice, the voice of a prophet. "Do you remember the Roman soldier's spear in our Savior's side?" he asks those of us in the cave and there is a murmur, heads bowed. "From that blow came this splinter. Where did you find it?" he asks Jehanne, setting the bone back in its kerchief, his eyes bright with understanding and divine light. I want to shout at the return of such a light and strength to his features. He is immortal. We are all immortal.

"In a chicken coop," Jehanne says. "From a cock who died in battle with another cock, a valiant but meaningless death."

She gathers up the leather kerchief from Domenic and shakes the bone onto the floor with a small laugh. "Grave robbers," she says. The monks, the children, the soldiers, even Jerome the idiot lose their looks of reverence and mill about us, the firelight dancing on the walls.

"Bastards," a soldier shouts and spits at me.

"Witches," says a boy and spits on Domenic.

"Devils," says an old woman and spits twice, once on each of us.

Spitting on heretics and blasphemers is one of the favorite pastimes in Chinon, but we're not heretics. We do the Lord's work. Domenic has fallen on his knees, his eyes closed, tears streaming down his face. Now he reaches in his tunic and holds his hands outstretched to Jehanne, shouting, "Here, here. This is a true relic, a true relic."

Jehanne puts up her arm and silences the crowd. She moves to take what he offers, though his grip is strong and he almost forgets to let her take it. He finally opens his hands to reveal a small bone, one that I do not recognize. It is yellow with age, long and thin, undoubtedly a human finger.

Jehanne takes the bone and examines it. Then she crosses herself and mutters a silent prayer.

"Where did you find this?" she asks him.

"I don't know," he says, crying and shaking his head. "I don't know. It appeared. It was the first. But no more came after this."

She smiles at him and says, "A true relic. A powerful and holy relic I will take with me to Rheims."

"But whose?" I ask her. "How do you know?"

She doesn't say.

The bones whisper doubt to me, not faith. This is what troubles me, how even the smartest kings and queens of the world determine with certainty the difference between God's voice and the voice of the serpent.

"Redeem yourself, Domenic," she says.

"Redeem them," one of the monks says with a sneer. "Redeem them both."

And that is all I hear except for a buzzing, growing louder and louder still until all other sound is drowned out. We're carried out of the cave by the crowd, and Domenic stumbles on a rock and falls. As he looks up, I graze his cheek with my hand.

Jehanne regards him, her face colorless, her lips as thin as a man's.

"Show him God's mercy," I say, lifting him up. Would that he could be borne to heaven now, but it is only I, Mathias, helping him to his feet.

"Redeem him," I beg.

"Redeem yourself," Jehanne says as she's helped up on her horse by the boy with the coat of arms stitched on his tunic.

Domenic looks at me tearfully. "She knows, she knows. We must follow her, father. She has been sent by the Lord to save us."

"You'll follow her, all right," says the boy, and there's laughter close to him and murmurs at the back of the group. "What did she say? What did she say?" They think it was Jehanne who spoke, but she has no trace of mirth. She looks away, shifts on her horse, and starts off.

Our hands are bound by soldiers. Her followers stuff our relics into sacks and tie these sacks by rope around our necks. And as we march into Chinon, the soldiers and townspeople sing, forgetting us. "Let each take his hoe, the better to uproot them. And if they do not wish to go, at least make a face at them. Do not fear to strike them, those big-bellied English soldiers, for one of us is worth four of them, or at least he is worth three of them."

Some voice or another is always whispering to me. Now it says, "Mathias, what have you done?" but it says no more. It repeats these words. I am a simple man and cannot interpret voices. I used to wonder how Domenic could be so certain of himself—even the nuns in Fontevraud recite the Holy Book without the slightest inflection, so afraid are they of adding their own interpretations to God's words.

Jehanne on her horse holds the finger of the Saint, her prize, in one hand while grasping her horse's rein in the other. The bone seems like a banner, towering invisible in its power into the clouds.

She circles back to me, regards me from her horse, and shows me the finger as if instructing me. But then she closes her hand around it and canters off. Did she show me this to torment me or to light the way?

"Show it to me, too," Domenic begs, as though he has never seen it before, though it has been in his possession for years.

Perhaps only our bodies imprison us, as the Cathars taught, and in each material object the divine spark glows. From the bones of the saints, the glow is constant. But what of the bones of ordinary men? If even the bones of the Saints lead us astray, then what good can they really be?

We stumble countless times as our bags of bones choke us when they stick on tree roots and rocks and brambles. But still, we drag them on, and they rattle and clamor as if they wish nothing more than to join in battle and in the songs of our redeemers.

Until I refuse to walk farther.

I wait in the dusty road, attentive to all sounds, all voices, a terrible thirst parching my throat. They walk on ahead of me, even Domenic, who joins Jehanne's followers in song as though

15

one of them. I wonder if he truly believes now or if he sings to save his mortal self.

The boy in the tunic moves to drag me, but I am much too heavy, so he beats me in the face with a switch.

Samuel, when he heard God's voice, thought it was Eli calling to him for help. After being awakened by Samuel three times, Eli understood and told Samuel what to say when God spoke.

This is what I try to say through the furious lashes of this boy.

"Speak, Lord, for your servant hears your call."

Magellan Stew

The following sixteenth-century diary was recently discovered among miscellaneous papers in the Rare Books Room at DePauw University in Greencastle, Indiana—once again changing what we thought we knew about history. It is the true account of Ferdinand Magellan's fateful battle with the forces of Datu Lapu-Lapu on Mactan island in 1521 in what is now the Philippines. The author, a Portuguese spy, most likely died along with twenty-six fellow officers, ambushed by the forces of Datu Raja Humabon only days after Magellan's death. Humabon and eight hundred of his followers had been converted to Christianity by Magellan, but angered by the Spanish crew's repeated abuse of the local women, Humabon's men ambushed the crew. The survivors retreated to their ships and made off for Spain, successfully circumnavigating the globe for the first time. One of the survivors, Juan Sebastian del Cano, took all the credit for Magellan's accomplishments, and it wasn't until centuries later that Magellan received his proper due, thanks to the discovery of the secret diary of Italian adventurer Antonio Pigafetta. It is not known how the present manuscript made its way to Indiana, or for certain the fate of its author. Perhaps he survived to live in exile on the island of Mactan or neighboring Cebu. This much is certain: he was not among the survivors who returned to Spain.—Editor's Note

The least enjoyable aspect of being a spy is that one can share so little of one's accomplishments. One knows this going into the profession, so I'm not complaining. Every great man disputes the history of others, makes his own maps, records his own borders, erects his own monuments. This holds equally true for all heroic men, men who were felled in their heroic quest, and those who but dreamed of heroics. The world is a collection of dreams and monuments to dreams. My monument is this chronicle, written on an island in the Portuguese hemisphere for no one's eyes but my own. Josafeta cannot read nor comprehend the designs of great nations, and I no longer wish to leave this island. So it alters nothing to proclaim that I can take some blame or reward, depending upon one's view, for the events that have transpired. My name is Paulo. It is my facility with languages that has made me so useful to Magellan as well as Emmanuel, King of Portugal. I am fluent in English, Spanish, Italian, German, Arabic, and of course, my native Portuguese. After three days with the Indios I could speak in sentences. After eight days, I could tell jokes and ghost stories, of which they share my fondness. After ten days, I had taken a native wife. I had her baptized and renamed her Josafeta. She is perhaps already sixteen, though thankfully, she looks much younger. It's difficult to tell for sure. She has many teeth, talks seldom, and her smell is pleasant like coconut, her skin dark and salty. No lice.

My mission will go partly unfulfilled—to report to my King the schemes and adventures of the Spanish, to make maps in secret, and to make my fellow countryman pay for his treason for ignoring the Treaty of Tordesillas. Clearly, the Spice Islands are east of Rome and by rights belong to the Portuguese, not the Spanish, who were awarded all that is west of Rome. The Spanish might laud him, but in Portugal, the land of his birth, he is roundly hated for his adventures. When Magellan asked King Emmanuel, his childhood playmate, to be released from his oath of allegiance so he could go where he wanted, the King told Magellan, "I don't care where you go. You can go to the devil." My opportunity to fulfill the King's suggestion finally came a few days ago when the Captain, having successfully converted eight hundred Indios in a single day to the true faith, turned his attentions to a village on a neighboring island, ruled by a chieftain named Lapu-Lapu. Contrary to his reputation, Lapu-Lapu was not so much warlike as curious—the Indios whom we had befriended, under the Christian chieftain, Raja Humabon, had told us to stay away from Lapu-Lapu, but this warning came perhaps out of self-interest as we had already blessed them with our superior ways, our medicines, our religion, our chocolate. They were not eager to share with their neighbors. Raja Humabon himself seemed of a greedy and indolent nature—we first encountered him, a short and fat man adorned with gold and tattoos, sitting on a mat gorging on turtles and palm wine which he sipped through a reed straw. Conversion, it seemed, was not new to this Chief or his people, as his name evidenced. The followers of Muhammed, slave traders mostly, had already sailed to this land, creating much havoc in this world and the next.

Lapu-Lapu sent an emissary to Raja Humabon's village, where we were billeted, to invite us to his village and host a feast in our honor. He said he would give us animals and foodstuffs. Magellan reacted favorably and asked me to convey that we would be happy to visit and that we would bring something that would change their lives forever for the better. I told the emissary, a young man all in tattoos, to tell the Chief that we would come, but only if he gave us twice as much as was offered. Otherwise, we would bring disease and calamity and change their lives forever.

One could tell by the emissary's glance that no one had ever spoken to Lapu-Lapu in this fashion. His stupefied expression Magellan mistook for one of gratitude.

The next day, he returned and said Lapu-Lapu would like us to leave. If we agreed, he would give us three times the number of foodstuffs, etc., that he had first offered.

"I'm afraid he rejects your gift," I told the Captain. "He says it's blasphemy of the blackest kind."

The Captain was a patient man and he told me to tell the Chief that the seas of his land were rich with fish, and while his people enjoyed the bounty of the seas on earth, they would starve in the afterlife if they did not bathe in the water of life and surrender to the fisher of souls.

It was a dreary speech; I'd had to translate it or its variants countless times, but it was well-spoken. The Captain's own words impressed himself deeply. He placed his hand to his chest and dreamily glanced at a cloud that had the shape of a dragon. I told the emissary that there was a certain delicious fish in these waters that we had named in honor of his Chief. I said we were a hungry people with great appetites and that we would eat Lapu-Lapu and his people and then we would eat the fish named after him and then we would drink the sea in which they swam, and still our appetites would not be quenched.

The emissary backed away quickly and fled over the sands. The next day we did not see him, but the day after that, he returned with another offer, this time double his last if we would leave and not return.

Magellan was waiting this time with a gift for the reluctant Chief, a Santo Nino much like the one he had presented to the wife of Raja Humabon.

"In the name of His Majesty, the King of Spain, Carlos, I present you with eternal life and salvation," the Captain said as he handed Lapu-Lapu's emissary a wooden statue of the Santo Nino for the Chief's veneration. The carving of the Christ child was indeed exquisite, its hand extended in blessing, on its face a look of such serenity that one would think the savior had indeed sat for modeling. But I am unlike most of my countrymen, Magellan included, who venerate such chunks of wood or plaster. I do not see

God in such likenesses, but always the hand of man. "Our leader, Magellan, wants Datu Lapu-Lapu to give him as many little boys as can be supplied," I told the young man. "Like this one."

The emissary narrowed his eyes and leaned forward. "*Gamay gna mga bata?*"

"Our Captain will make them into a stew," I said. "It's very delicious. We call it paella."

"*Gago gyud!*" the man said presently.

And indeed, the young man was right. The Captain was crazy.

"Did you say paella?" Magellan asked me.

As with any battle, the moments before it commenced were glorious. Before me, dense foliage spilled to the white beach. Overhead, gulls floated and three black long-billed birds silently crossed the skies above the beach like sentries hurrying off in warning. Above the gentle waves, the forest sounds cascaded, but if I listened carefully, I could distinguish one from the other: the monkey, the one-word language of the gecko—"Too-ko!"—the flutes and whistles and hoarse cries of birds yet unseen, and the clamor of insects. The hostile Indios, arrayed along the beach in their finery, in their bark cloth and tattoos, pounded their shields and yelled taunts at us. Perhaps two thousand of them faced us. No one was particularly concerned about their numbers. Magellan had even granted Lapu-Lapu an extra day to prepare for battle and draw up a sizeable force and prepare enough spears and poison arrows to meet us. This worried no one. All Magellan really needed was his cannon, but I had long ago observed something about Magellan that made me fairly confident that this battle would be his undoing: his total lack of interest in conquest. Oh, he made a show of it from time to time, but one could see it was all an act. For months now he had been defying his orders and instead of nailing the Spanish crest everywhere he went, he had been planting crosses. Not in itself a crime, but not what young King Carlos had sent him to do. Thus far, he had only fired our cannon in these islands to impress the natives and had only worn armor for fighting demonstrations.

Still Magellan was sure that God would help him defeat the Indios, even if he went at them alone, which he nearly did. I can claim some responsibility for this set of circumstances as well. After Lapu-Lapu's emissary departed for the last time, I told the Captain that the Indios planned to make a stew of him. To this, the Captain laughed, one of the few times I have heard laughter from him. "Very well then," he said, rubbing his beard as though it irritated him. "We will see who makes the water boil."

It was that night that he had a vision. He did not go into details, but the next day he asked for the cooks and stewards to be assembled on deck. His faith, he told them, was very strong. God had plans for these islands, great plans that would not be known for hundreds of years. If they wanted to be part of God's design, he told them, they would follow him. Another dreary speech, but it impressed the cooks.

As we approached Lapu-Lapu's island on the appointed day, our ships could not get close enough to the shore for the cannon to be effective against the Chief, who had withdrawn his forces past the high-water mark. A wide coral reef in shallow waters blocked our advancement. This dissuaded Magellan little. He and his force strode down the gangplank into waist-deep water, Magellan carrying his lance in one hand. He walked, as always, with a pronounced limp, but when he hit the water he pressed forward as though no human frailty could keep him from his appointed task. Behind him rushed a rabble of cooks, cabin boys, and stewards, ungainly in their borrowed armor. Many hadn't even fired a gun before or leveled a crossbow or raised a blade above their head except to cut through a shank of lamb. Still, they were an enthusiastic group, not bloodthirsty enough perhaps, but naively eager, as though the heathen Indios could be rounded up like so many loose hens, their heads chopped off, their feathers plucked. A couple of idiots plunged into the water with great war cries, fell backward, and never rose again in this life, weighed down by their armor. The rest tipped forward awkwardly.

Unless one was there, one could scarcely believe that Magellan had emptied the galleys of our food preparers to meet the Indios. But it was so—along with several officers, who had begged the Captain to accompany him into battle. Most who remained, including myself, lined the decks of our remaining two ships, passing around our spyglasses and bottles of drink, and swatting the mosquitoes that swarmed us. The cynical among our number, nearly all (after our hardships—the storms, the mutinies, the privations), laid bets and muttered their curses and hopes that the Captain would find his way into some native's stew pot, but no one believed such a fate could truly befall him, not with our cannon in support. While the officers and marines debated the merits of the Captain's present campaign, that ass-kissing Italian tourist, Pigafetta, danced around on the deck with his spyglass, pausing sometimes to mop his forehead or wring his hands and cry out gaudily to the Lord to protect "our true guide, the light of our lives."

The friendly Indios the Captain had converted looked on from their canoes which ringed our ships, eager to see their enemy defeated with Christ's help. The Captain was still out of range of the Indio bamboo spears and arrows, the Indios out of range of our mortars and crossbows. Defeat and victory hovered side by side like the heat and mosquitoes. In the water, schools of bright fish swarmed, and for a moment, I forgot my place in the current drama, and was only moved by the Lord's bounty. Surely, the seas and jungles of the world are infinite, I thought. The Lord has given them to us to tame, but that will not happen in a thousand lifetimes.

The battle commenced with the cabin boys leveling their cross-bows and shooting two of our best cooks in the back. The remaining cooks responded with hearty oaths and curses and turned and fired upon the cabin boys. Not one cabin boy was hit, but a steward was hit in the arm and began to cry. Magellan's troops had not fired one shot at the Indios, but had already been reduced to forty-five men, a fact that escaped no one's notice. Our forces looked on silently now while Lapu-Lapu's men pounded their shields and laughed and shouted. Poor Magellan strode among his men, ordering them to spread out and move forward. They moved forward for a minute, then froze as the first Indios' arrows landed in front of them. Without orders, they responded in kind, firing without regard. For nearly ten minutes, the cooks fired uselessly at the Indios, well out of range, while we stood at the rails and groaned or shook our heads. Magellan, we could see, was striding among them, telling them to cease fire, but most of these servants, in a mixture of terror and sudden power, would not cease. At the close of this spectacle, the Indios, not one of them having been felled, massed and charged into the water.

Several more of the officers had decided to join battle and come to their Captain's aid. I jumped onto the gangplank and ran with them, hardly aware of what I was doing. Pigafetta leaned over the ship's rails, tossed me a crossbow and quiver, and yelled encouragement. I offered that he should join us, but he shook his head and indicated a bad back.

The cooks, much terrified, turned around and ran through the shallow water, over the corals, from which they received many injuries. Only the Captain and ten faithful officers and stewards stood their ground. The remaining officers, now much alarmed, quickly made ready with the cannon. They fired a volley, and for a moment the Indios paused and watched the smoke from our ships and the mortars, well out of range, drop uselessly on the coral beds between the opposing sides. The ships could maneuver no closer, but the cannons were reloaded as though the wishes of the crew could propel their mortars farther.

The friendly Indios, gathered around our boats, could stand the spectacle no longer and rushed forward, faster than we, encumbered as we were by our armor. But before they could meet their enemies, another cannon volley sailed into their midst, killing four instantly and changing the minds of the others. The friendly Indios were now unfriendly Indios and they rushed back toward us.

All this confused Lapu-Lapu's forces, and for a moment they stopped fighting. They hardly knew what to think of a force that insisted on repeatedly attacking itself.

Then their houses started to burn. Magellan had sent a small force to set their village on fire as a diversion. This would not have been a bad idea under normal circumstances, but now the Indios, further enraged, massed as one and drove toward Magellan.

None of this had a salutary effect on me or those who had joined in the Captain's aid. As fast as we had come, we began to withdraw while the Captain and a few of his men fought on. The Captain waded ahead while the natives shot their spears and arrows only at his legs. He slashed at them with his sword and they threw their spears at him and then, pressing forward as they pressed him back, picked them up and threw again. An Indio made to attack him with a sword like a scimitar and the Captain impaled him with his lance, which stuck in his body. Magellan made to withdraw his sword, but his arm had been injured and was no use. An arrow struck him in the foot. He grasped it and wrenched it out, but he gave one last look toward us and the ship. He yelled something I could not decipher and then his head was pushed under water and I could not bear to watch anymore as he and the unlucky few at his side were buried under a thrashing sea of Indios.

Walking the beach today, I found a shred of Magellan—not a shred really, more like a hunk of linguisa sausage, the Captain's favorite, something he missed from his native land. I was with Josafeta, holding her hand, and humming a hymn, trying to explain to myself the fullness of my heart. Magellan is dead, and for this I am truly sad. To be the translator of a great man is to be both the humblest of servants and most exalted among men. Whatever truths are not lost in the tumult of time as it crashes cruelly around us, we speak as dull echoes amid the constant din. We make of others' words what we will, we reinterpret, we make our own designs, and thus change our fates and the fates of generations.

Raja Humabon, as it turns out, is not so bad a figure of a man after all. He was quick to forgive the loss of his men from our cannon and some rough treatment of the local women by some of our crew. Last night, we toasted our brave Captain and ate Lapu-Lapu—I have told them of Magellan's final insult to the Chief, which was really mine, and they have adopted the name for their local fish with great pleasure. It will always be thus with the vanquished: their revenge is enacted with insults and rude jokes. Tonight, Humabon has invited us to another feast.

Last night, I had a vision of sorts, too. In the West, I saw a great cross, and in the east I saw fire. When I looked behind me, I saw the Captain, dying, his forehead caressed by the Mother of God. In front of me, I saw a heart frozen within a snowy chalice. I cannot say whether it was my heart in that chalice, and if it was, what made it thaw. Perhaps loneliness. I awoke trembling in Josafeta's arms. The vision, I suppose, is open to interpretation, and I tried to relate it to Josafeta, who was of little help and seemed interested only in my definition of snow.

Local Time

I

"Shoot me if I ever get old," E.K. told Stribley as they left the taxi and entered one of the clubs that lined both sides of the street. The place was called Dodge City. To Stribley, E.K. was already old, even grandfatherly in bearing, but he had a youthful smile and energetic eyes.

They entered a cavernous room bursting with strobe lights briefly illuminating small packs of white men and Asians facing a stage where women were dressed in cowgirl outfits. Some of the women wore white hats and some black, and all had holsters. Some had their tops off, some more than that. Some wore only holsters. All wore stiletto cowboy boots. That's where the Western theme ended.

They sat at an empty table and a swarm of girls from the stage and all corners of the room milled around them, three finally taking seats beside them. A waitress appeared and E.K. ordered San Miguel beers for both of them and the three women ordered tequilas and ice teas.

E.K. considered Stribley one of the firm's more promising younger associates—that's what he told him when he offered him the opportunity to come along. E.K. had done his mission in the Philippines thirty years ago and had been coming back ever since. He looked to be in his late fifties now, or early sixties; he still had a full head of hair, and a beard streaked in three different colors: white, silver, and a smidgeon of black. The beard was well trimmed, but it was nearly the length of a prophet's. In Salt Lake City, E.K. seemed the model of propriety. He drank occasionally but he didn't smoke and the harshest curse he uttered in public was "Heck!" At the company picnic, E.K. had teared up when speaking of his experience volunteering for Habitat for Humanity.

"What are we doing here?" Stribley asked presently.

"Staying awake. Staying alive. Getting on local time."

Every ten minutes, the women were served drinks and a waitress came over and asked E.K. to sign a slip, which he did each time, studying the slip of paper scrupulously before signing it.

Stribley's girl, if you could call her that—she seemed to think she was his girl—hung on his shoulder and smiled at him. He suspected she didn't speak English.

They had meetings scheduled tomorrow morning. "Hit the ground running" was E.K.'s motto. All Stribley could imagine was the feel of a pillow cushioning his head. "Shouldn't we be up early?" Stribley asked.

"Early? Hell, it *is* early and we're up. Relax. You're half a world away from all your worries."

The Salt Lake City marketing agency Stribley and E.K. worked for promoted, among other things, apples from Utah. People didn't usually associate apples with Utah, which was something E.K.'s firm had been hired to correct. Washington apples had more or less cornered the Philippine market, and some Fuji apples from Japan, but Washington sent apples too old for the domestic market to the Philippines. Filipinos, E.K. said, deserved better apples, not these desiccated things that looked like apples but tasted like Brazil nuts. Filipinos, following Chinese tradition, gave round fruits on Christmas and New Year's; the roundness of the fruit signified prosperity, and apple sales did well around these times. If he could convince the major Philippine chains to take on Utah apples, the potential market was staggering.

"I'm going back to the hotel," Stribley said. Standing, he faltered, feeling a wave of stupefying fatigue the likes of which he'd never before experienced.

"No wait, I'll come with you."

Somehow, instead of leading E.K. to a taxi, Stribley found himself following E.K. down a hill to a health club, which wasn't a health club at all. Here, women were displayed behind glass in a room the size of a nursery for newborns. E.K. suggested he pick one.

"Pick one?"

"Or two."

"Give him that one," E.K. said presently to a skinny young man who stood between them.

Her number was 66. One more six and it would have been 666, the sign of the Beast, Stribley fretted as she lay on top of him fifteen minutes later. She gazed as with undying love and sang a Karen Carpenter song: "I'm on the top of the world, looking down on creation."

"What? You don't like my singing, Sir?" He hadn't even realized he was laughing. Every time he touched her, she moaned. He touched her breast with a kind of E.T. or Michelangelo tentativeness and she moaned. He put his hand on her neck and she heaved a passionate breath. He tried touching her forehead. Nothing.

"If you come back, remember my number, darling." She whispered it in his ear. And the next thing he knew he was waking up without having realized he'd fallen asleep, being bundled out the door by two men, one of whom he thought was E.K. 66 handed him his wallet and she said, "Be careful," then sang, "Why do birds suddenly appear every time you are near?"

He called up Rikki afterward just to hear her voice and vowed to himself he'd never do such a stupid thing again. "This place is a pit," he told her.

"Oh, my poor honey. Well, chin up and come home soon. Here, Matthew wants to sing his number from the spring pageant." She handed Matthew the phone. "All the birds sing words and the flowers croon in the Tiki Tiki Tiki Tiki Tiki Room!" the boy shouted without warning or much in the way of melody.

By the end of the song, Stribley found it difficult to breathe. It was an awful song, a tragic song. "That's lovely," he told Matthew. But never again would he be able to hear the Tiki Room song without thinking melancholy thoughts. He'd been away only one day and had broken his wedding vows. He'd broken his son's heart and his son didn't even know it.

The next morning he found a note from her in his underwear. "Even though you're ten thousand miles away, I feel you near me."

He put his head in his hands and wept until the phone by his bed rang. It was E.K. "Wake up, wake up," E.K. shouted.

"I'm up," Stribley said glumly. "When's our first meeting?"

"Canceled," E.K. said. "How do you like them apples?"

"What do you mean, canceled?" Stribley asked.

"That's just how things work here," E.K. said.

E.K., undeterred, made appointments for the following day with similar results. The people they were supposed to meet were never where they said they would be. E.K. said they'd have to stay at least another week. This just called for a change of strategy. When E.K. learned that the daughter of the General Manager of Robinson's Supermarket was getting married, he had ten boxes of apples delivered to the wedding reception at the Manila Polo Club. The next day they were finally able to meet with the General Manager, Mr. Samuel Ong, a Filipino of Chinese descent, at his office in Makati, near their hotel.

"You know," Mr. Ong said, sitting across from them at his massive desk made from a kind of wood that Stribley had never heard of, "I like your apples, but no one knows Utah here. Except for the

Utah Jazz. Maybe we could call them Utah Jazz apples. Everyone likes the Jazz. Karl Malone. John Stockton. It's a matter of name recognition here in the Philippines more than the actual taste, which as I said is quite good."

Stribley waited for either Mr. Ong or E.K. to laugh, but the two looked at each other like men with apple empires to build. E.K. stroked his beard and said, "Utah Jazz apples!"

Mr. Ong asked if they had brought any more apples and E.K. said sure, we have loads of apples. Mr. Ong had a board meeting and he wanted to give a box to each of his board members. "A splendid idea," E.K. said.

"We can't call them Utah Jazz apples," Stribley said on the elevator ride down.

"I know that," E.K. said. "I'm just being culturally sensitive."

"So what was going on in there?"

"Hard to tell," said E.K. "Most likely, we just gave away a lot of apples."

But it didn't seem to faze E.K. in the least. Every night he visited the bars, and every day he dragged Stribley to one canceled appointment or fruitless (so to speak) meeting after another. After that first night, Stribley avoided accompanying E.K. on his nightly outings. Each day, he found a new note in his suitcase, sometimes in his socks, sometimes in his underwear, once in a pocket of a shirt. Each was a variation on the same theme—"I miss you. I can't wait until you're home." He wanted to go home, too, but he also knew that he'd have to face Rikki with what he'd done. To her, keeping a secret was worse than acting badly, and they had always solemnly told each other their darkest truths.

Full disclosure was the bedrock of their marriage. When Rikki found a hundred dollars on the floor by a co-worker's teller window, she had pocketed it and then soberly confessed her crime to Stribley later that night. She was trembling when she told him. She was too humiliated for anyone else to know, but she insisted he be her accomplice. Emboldened, Stribley had taken her confession as permission to admit an affair from the first year of their marriage, an old girlfriend who came suddenly back into his life. To his surprise, Rikki reacted badly, threatening to kick him out of the house and ruin him financially. Two days later, she came around, but she told him not to count on it next time. The ground rules still applied. Confess or live alone with your crime, in orbit around the intimacy of marriage, but never truly intimate again.

"What about the money you took from the bank?" he said.

"It's bad," she said. "I know. But I'm not married to the bank. I can live with being emotionally estranged from the bank." He wondered now what was really behind her notes. Maybe they were simply reminders. Maybe she knew she couldn't trust him. This put Stribley in an odd frame of mind. On the one hand, she was right. Apparently, as his experience with 66 attested, he couldn't be trusted. But he wanted to think he was within reach of being completely trustworthy. He resented Rikki's assumption that he wasn't.

Perhaps Stribley's odd frame of mind had more to do with being completely unprepared for this trip rather than with the cornucopia of mildly antic love notes from Rikki. Outside the confines of the business district—Makati, with its upscale shopping malls and five-star hotels—the city seemed an endless warren of slums and traffic jams. Squatters' areas crammed every available space, even along railroad tracks, with slapdash huts of corrugated metal and boards piled up like anthills; scrawny dogs and scrawny children; people living under bridges and overpasses; pawnshops and tiny shops called sari-sari stores, fast-food chains, 7-Elevens, gas stations; mechanics that advertised "vulcanizing" and aircon repair; smoke-belching buses from a hundred different bus companies changing lanes wildly, charging heedlessly into intersections; the silver local buses called jeepneys; neighborhoods of high walls topped by glass and barbed wire; a peek, through a gate at which an armed guard slept, of a garden, a swimming pool, while outside the gated mansions garbage scattered across broken sidewalks; the charred ruins of a sports complex slowly crumbled, not knocked down but simply incorporated into some sprawling squatter-constructed outer building; buildings were going up or down or simply sat abandoned, nearly impossible to tell the difference; massive churches rose from slums; skeletal palm trees struggled alongside giant concrete abutments; hand-painted billboards in Tagalog advertised Barbara Milano in *Kaulayaw* and Jackie Woo in *Hustler;* and everywhere karaoke bars and "short-time" hotels suggested pleasure by way of the black-and-white silhouette of a woman with her finger in front of her mouth.

"When are we going home?" Stribley asked E.K. one day when he showed up once again at Stribley's door, urging his protégé to join him in a night of carousing. E.K. wore a tee shirt that read: "The reason why I can't wear shorts." Underneath this caption was a cartoon of a man remarkably similar to E.K. in build, whose penis and testicles dangled below his shorts. The day before, E.K. wore a tee shirt with the Pepsi logo, altered to read PENIS, and the day before that, a MasterCard logo with the word MASTURBATE instead. With every passing day, E.K. grew more and more depraved. Was this the same guy he'd worked for the past eleven months, whose walls were decorated with photos of his children and grandchildren? Stribley vowed to go on the job market as soon as he returned to Salt Lake.

"We've got another two weeks here at least. Mr. Ong wants twenty-four more crates delivered."

For a moment, there was silence. Then he heard E.K. pad away. He stood at the door reading the emergency exit instructions, the room rates, the checkout time. Presently, he heard footsteps again and E.K.'s voice, hitched up a notch. "Listen, tomorrow morning I'm going to Angeles for a few days. You can wait here for the apples to be delivered. Man, you're a wet blanket."

Stribley kept reading the hotel rules, silently mouthing them as though they formed an age-old prayer. Angeles was a city of girlie bars a couple hours' drive from Manila, not far from the old U.S. airbase, Clark Field. Every other cabbie offered to bring him there.

The next day he called up FedEx and asked when he could expect the apple shipment, then he spent the rest of the day in a daze wandering through crowds in one of the malls. That night, he searched through the rest of his luggage for more notes from Rikki, but he'd apparently found them all. He really needed a note right now. She was at work. He couldn't call her. So he sat in his underwear in front of the TV flipping through the channels.

He stopped at a karaoke channel where words panned underneath videos that seemed to have nothing to do with the words. In one video, sailboats plied a river that seemed to be somewhere in Europe. A group of very blonde people raised and lowered sails. He sang along. "Just like me, they long to be close to you!"

As long as nothing happened, Stribley figured a little nightlife was okay. Of course, something had already happened with 66, but that had been his first night, he'd not been on his guard, he'd been in a stupor. He should stop torturing himself. He should forget that. As long as he didn't act on his impulses, he'd be okay. And if worse came to worst and he acted, well, he'd already fouled up that first night, so in a way that was almost a justification for fouling up again. He already felt guilty about 66, and he couldn't go back and undo what he'd done, so doing it again would make his guilt stronger, which would push him over the edge into good behavior once again. That was how he worked. A good kick in the pants always gave him perspective and renewed his resolve to be a good guy.

What the hell. He got dressed and caught a taxi.

II

The mamasan sat down with him, a woman named Gemma in her mid-twenties with wide eyes and high cheekbones. She asked him to buy her a drink, but drank it slowly and didn't pressure him.

"Where did you learn English?" he asked. "It's good. You don't even have an accent."

"The States. I went to school there. My dad lives in San Francisco."

"So why are you working here?" He regretted asking the question, but it had slipped out. Someone who was obviously educated and smart had other options. "I mean," he said, trying to recover, "why work here in the Philippines and not in the States, where your dad lives?'

"Circumstances," she said. "*Kapit sa patalim.*"

"What does that mean?"

"It means hanging on by the blade."

"The blade?"

"Here, I have a dagger in my hand," she said. "It's very sharp, so sharp that the slightest touch will break skin and your blood will pour out. Now grab it."

She tightly clutched an invisible blade.

He touched her hand and she drew back as though he'd cut her. Then slowly, she offered him the invisible knife. "Not my hand," she said. "The blade."

He wondered if she was crazy, but at the same time, he felt intrigued.

"Now why would I want to grab hold of a very sharp blade?"

"It's not a matter of wanting," she said, spreading wide the fingers that had previously grasped the invisible knife. "*Kapit sa patalim.*"

The lights from the stage flashed on her face, making her expression go in and out of shadow. "If you're thinking of fucking me," she said, "I'm not going to fuck you, okay?"

"I wasn't thinking that."

"Almost anyone else in here, okay, but not me. Filipino women," she said, as though he had asked her a question, "don't have strong personalities. They're easy to manipulate. They fall for any line."

"Really?" he said. "How can you say that about all Filipino women?"

"Not all," she said. "But many. The majority. I can say it because I know."

He sat with Gemma for a few minutes drinking his beer. Why had he refused to accompany E.K. on his nightly prowls, but then returned as soon as E.K. left town? He couldn't answer. But he and E.K. were not the same, and his being here did not mean that he was going to start wearing PENIS shirts tomorrow. He didn't want to manipulate anyone.

"Have any plans to return to the States, Gemma?" he asked, as though he might offer her a visa. But really he just wanted to say something because saying nothing made his conscience take a slow stroll down Stribley Lane, which now seemed strewn with stray bits of litter.

"Can't," she said.

"Circumstances?"

She gave that some thought. "I was married to an asshole. I don't want him to find me or my daughter."

"Oh, you've got a daughter? I have a son." The music grew louder, a frantic bleating backed up by a bass line that sent defibrillating shock waves through Stribley.

"Mayday is known to him," she said.

"What?"

She cupped her hands. "Maybe you should moan to him."

"I can't hear you. I'm sorry."

Onstage, women danced to "It's Raining Men" as they twirled umbrellas between their legs with equal amounts of suggestiveness, clumsiness, and boredom.

"What do you think of Manila?" she asked after the song had ended. The girls left the stage, a shift change.

It's crowded and dirty, he wanted to say. "I haven't had a chance to see much of it," he said. "Truthfully," he added, "I haven't really felt like myself since I've been here."

She laughed. "And how do you usually feel?"

"I miss my son." He took a photo from his wallet and handed it to her like a passport. Her mood seemed to change as she studied it carefully. "Ah, *gwapo*," she said admiringly. "What a handsome boy!"

As she handed back the photo, she seemed to study Stribley for a moment and he felt a shiver. She looked at him with an expression he read as caring, or maybe something more complicated than that; whatever it was was tinged with sadness. His beer made a watermark on the table, which he circled with his finger. "Would you like a tour?" she asked. "I have tomorrow off."

Maybe you should go home to him. That's what she had been saying.

And this is certainly what he should have done, but her saying this, and all of those things she said about hanging on by the blade made him weaken in a way he couldn't quite understand. Call it tenderness, call it sentiment, or a sense of power and privilege masquerading as pity. Whatever it was, it grabbed him, as they say, by the balls.

III

Stribley sat with Gemma in the back of the cab, she on one side, he on the other. The ride from Makati to Roxas Boulevard along Manila Bay took almost forty-five minutes—she chatted nearly the entire way as though she really were a tour guide and not a mamasan, manically pointing out the sights.

The cab driver, a man with gray hair and a red and gold Chinese money charm hanging from his rearview, glanced back at them, chuckling every so often at one of Gemma's remarks, making no pretense of minding his own business.

"Do you have any children, Sir?" the driver asked.

"One," Stribley said. "A boy."

"Only one," he said. "That's too bad. I have seven. You know, Sir. One's first child is a miracle. One's second child is an achievement. After that, it's a habit."

Stribley laughed and Gemma smiled sadly and scooted a little closer to the window. She didn't speak—her tour guide persona seemed momentarily depleted, and her melancholy passed from her to him like a germ. He thought of Matthew, tried to imagine what his son was doing, but he'd lost track of the time difference. What time was it now? Was it fourteen hours' difference or fifteen hours', and what day was it? A fissure of something like grief or maybe revulsion opened in him and he looked away and tried to focus on what was in front of him, a statue of some local hero.

"Can you tell me who he is?" Stribley asked Gemma feebly, as though he were speaking of someone who'd been in a terrible accident.

"That's our national hero," she said. "José Rizal."

"Do you know why they have a guard in front of his statue, Sir?" the cabbie asked Stribley.

"No, why?"

"So he won't leave and go to the bars in Makati."

Stribley laughed and so did Gemma. Both laughs surprised him. He found something charming about the cabbie's irreverence. In Americans like E.K., this carnal honesty seemed merely grotesque, but these Filipinos wore it with, well, a certain dignity. Who would say such a thing while passing a statue of Washington? In America, people were statues, while here even statues seemed human.

Despite his first impressions of the city, Stribley soon discovered in Gemma's company that Manila had its charms if one was patient. After a visit to the National Museum, where they viewed recovered shipwrecks and tribal artifacts and paintings by the country's masters, they took another taxi to the oldest part of

Manila, the walled citadel of Intramuros. This was what Stribley had imagined Manila should look like, a quaint fortress with cobbled streets, ancient cathedrals, and horse-drawn carriages. Here, they dined in a quiet courtyard restaurant on gambas al ajillo, Spanish sardines, jamón de Serrano, and calamansi juice. Stribley complimented Gemma on her taste and her talent as a tour guide.

"I love my country," she said, dipping a piece of bread in a swirl of olive oil, garlic, and hot peppers. "I like to show off its good points. You know, we have 7,107 islands—at least at low tide."

"And how many have you been to?" Stribley asked.

"One only," she said, plucking a piece of dough from the center of her bread as though this morsel she held in her hands were the island she spoke of. Instead of eating it, she dropped it on the table and a look of resignation marred her face. "I used to say I was going to visit 10 percent of all the islands in my lifetime, but I don't even think I'll visit 1 percent now. I'm old already. I'm twenty-eight."

"Old?" Stribley said, laughing. He reached across the table and took her hand. He hadn't meant to do this exactly, but when he felt her tighten her fingers around his, he felt something so strong and sudden rush through him that it seemed as though he might physically lift up and levitate.

"If you could visit one other island, which would you like to see most?" he asked.

"That's easy. Boracay."

That evening, he returned to the Shangri-La to find a room laden with twenty-four crates of apples. Stubbing his toe on one of the crates, he hopped around the room as though doing a mating dance for Gemma. She sat on the bed laughing.

"Damn, E.K.!" he shouted.

"You have to be careful," Gemma told him when he finally came to a landing, and she rubbed his toe tenderly as they sat on the bed.

IV

Asian Spirit, the airline was called. After you crashed, that's what you'd be, he told Gemma: an Asian spirit. Hey, Stribley was getting the hang of it. But he truly felt frightened as the cabin filled with smoke. Not smoke really, but condensation from the air conditioning. As the flight attendant sat down, she crossed herself and Stribley pointed this out to Gemma. "Maybe she knows something we don't," he said. This time, Gemma took him seriously. "It doesn't mean anything," she said. "We always ask God for a blessing before a trip so that nothing bad will happen."

As the plane took to the sky. Stribley hypnotized himself with the view out the window, the sun glittering below on scores of fish pens that trailed into the sea along the city's coast.

Not more than an hour later, they landed at the small airfield on Panay, an island that neighbored Boracay, where they were met by a throng of tricycle drivers, one separating himself from the others and claiming Stribley and Gemma's luggage. After a short and noisy ride in the cramped tricycle, they boarded a *banca,* a motorized outrigger that brought them to Boracay, or at least most of the way. The *banca* stopped a hundred feet or so from shore and a group of skinny porters waded out to carry luggage and passengers alike. A boy half his size wanted to ferry Stribley on his back—the boy pointed to Stribley's shoes and long pants. But it seemed ridiculous—he'd crush the boy. "It's okay," Gemma said. "Filipinos are used to hard work. And it's how he makes his living." Remarkably, the boy managed to carry Stribley without even a grimace or a grunt. "How much should I tip him?" Stribley asked Gemma, who herself was astride a boy even smaller than Stribley's. The two boys seemed to be racing to shore, both smiling fiercely and watching one another as though the people on their backs didn't exist. "*Bahala ka,*" Gemma shouted back.

"I don't know what that means."

"It means it's up to you," she said.

And so it *was* up to him, although he had no idea what that meant. Certainly, there was precedent. Certainly, there was an accepted model of behavior in situations such as this, a certain amount one was expected to tip, but no one would tell him. No one would tell him anything, least of all E.K., who could at least have been decent enough to warn him that one of these days he was going to find himself racing on the back of a Filipino boy to the shores of a tropical island in the company of a beautiful woman who was not his wife. Surely, E.K. could have seen this would happen and could at least have given him a heads-up. It's one thing to find out that your boss is a stranger, a dirty old man who's been passing himself off as an upstanding member of the community, but to find out that you're a stranger to yourself, that you're capable of the most shocking behavior, is another thing entirely. *Bahala ka,* indeed. But who was this "you" it was up to?

Their hotel, called Cloud Nine, faced the ocean, a short jaunt from the boat station where Stribley and Gemma had landed. A dozen or so huts outfitted with air conditioning and mini bars faced a copse of palms giving way to white sand beach and the calmest turquoise water Stribley had ever seen. Their hut, as it turned out, was in the first line facing the sea, and a feeling almost like the one he had experienced when he first took Gemma's hand swept over him.

After they signed in, Gemma flopped on the bed and smiled. "Boracay," she said. "Have you ever seen such fine white sand? They say this is the most beautiful beach in the world." She withdrew her cell phone from her purse and called her daughter Mia. For a moment, Stribley watched her giddily as she spoke a mix of Tagalog and English to the little girl, who lived with Gemma's mother in Pampanga. Stifling his own urge to call home, Stribley went outside and sucked in the breeze as though sucking a cigarette, his lungs full of a pleasure he knew might eventually kill him.

When Gemma burst out of the room smiling, he could see tear tracks, but pretended not to notice. She beamed exuberantly. "Let's go. I want a picture by the water."

Stribley had brought his camera with him and he took a dozen photos of Gemma beneath a palm tree, sitting on the palm tree, pretending to hold up the palm tree, which was bent and looked like it might topple on her.

They walked the tourist paths, where hawkers tried to interest them in everything from elaborate wooden models of sailing ships to fake designer sunglasses while in the near distance motorcycle taxis whined up and down the streets behind the resorts. Although Gemma had never before been to Boracay, she knew what to look for and led him down an alley crowded with shops until they arrived at a restaurant where you picked out your fish and were given a choice of how it was prepared. They sat on the second floor, fans blowing hot air on them, drinking Coke after Coke from little bottles with straws. Gemma poured soy sauce in a little bowl, then squeezed calamansi into the soy, tore pieces of fish, added some rice, dipped it into the sauce and ate it with her hands. "That's the way we do it here," she said. Stribley tried it, and somehow the fish tasted more flavorful and delicate than any he'd ever tasted.

As he reached into his pocket to pay for the meal, he felt a piece of paper and pulled it out. Unfolding it, he felt a sudden dread. The paper was a note from Rikki. How had he missed it? It read, "Know that I'm always with you." It felt like an extortion note.

"What is it?" Gemma asked.

"A note from my wife," he said, crumpling it, thinking the afternoon was ruined now.

"I also have one from my husband in San Francisco," and she reached into her pocket.

"Really?" Stribley asked.

"No. It's a joke only. But sometimes I feel that he can see me, that he's going to catch up with me, and he won't let me be happy. Life can be so sweet. That's all I want, to taste a little of life's sweetness."

"What about now? Does it taste sweet?"

She reached for a thin napkin as it skittered off the table in a gust of air blown by the fan. "Yes," she said, letting the one go and reaching for another.

Outside, Gemma shopped for a sarong and for *pasolubong*, souvenirs for her friends back in Manila, key rings that said "Boracay" and puka shell bracelets. While she looked around, Stribley sneaked into an adjacent shop and purchased a small bag of seashells so delicate and fine, they looked too perfect to have been formed naturally. But somewhere, on some true paradise remoter than Boracay, such shells could still be found. Such amazing homes these creatures had. He had never actually seen what lived inside—some sea blob or another, unaware of the beauty it surrounded itself with. He opened the bag of shells and placed them carefully in his pockets, his loose shirt covering the bulges.

A monkey was tied to the roof of the shop where he'd purchased his shells, and he stopped to pity it, but he was the only one. He wanted to go inside and purchase the monkey, bring it to the hills and free it. He imagined it wandering into the bush, turning around and saluting him in gratitude before vanishing into the jungle canopy forever.

"What are you looking at?" Gemma said, grabbing his arm. "You look crazy just standing here with your mouth open."

"A monkey. See it?"

"Ai, it's so dirty," she said as though he were a boy to be chided for straying too close to a wild creature.

A tendril of regret choked him. He had hoped he might fall in love with Gemma, but his feelings flaked away with every word she spoke. Her accent seemed somehow stronger now. He wished there were some good way out of this, not that she seemed to expect anything of him, but he had expected more from himself. All he wanted now was to be home with his wife and son. He risked so many things by being with her: his family, his health, his self-respect. All he could think of was how to quietly and quickly end this situation.

That night, they strolled down the beach hand-in-hand past sand castles illumined by candles. Children stood by these creations and as they passed, the kids approached and stuck out their hands. "Donation, donation," they said. The castles looked lovely, amazing to have been created by such small hands, but the children made him wary. He just wanted a moonlight stroll, not another transaction, not another attempt to wrest him from his money. This thought, in turn, worried him. He didn't want to be the kind of callous American E.K. was, but he also recognized he was starting to act like the counterpart to E.K., the legendary ugly American who soothed his own ego with his purchasing power. Why had he given those boys so much money that afternoon? Why had he fantasized about buying the monkey at the store and freeing it? Such a pathetic and unrealistic fantasy. Why had he brought Gemma to Boracay? But he thought perhaps that was the nature of his life, that part of his struggle was to determine what was real, if anything. He saw his life as a kind of roiling surf, so unlike the calm shore of Boracay. Wading out, he was battered by successive waves of fantasy, each one submerging him, tossing him about, before he struggled to his feet and tried again.

Gemma scanned the beach in front of her as they walked, looking for seashells. Stribley wore a flashlight on his head, a device solemnly given to him by his father-in-law before Stribley left the States. The old man had been stationed at Subic during Vietnam and acted as though Stribley might have to escape Communist guerrillas in the dead of night. "This is better than a flashlight," he said. "Lets you keep your hands free." And it did, though every time he turned to Gemma to speak with her he momentarily blinded her with the beam. Now he withdrew one of the fine shells he'd purchased and tossed it to his side a few feet ahead. Then he trained his light on it. "There's one!" he shouted.

Gemma ran over to it and picked it up. "Oh my God," she said. "This is beautiful. This is perfect. Mia will love it."

As she turned it over in her hands, admiring its perfection, Stribley took another shell from his pocket and tossed it in front of him. "There's another!" he shouted and she ran over and picked this one up, too. "Can you believe it?" she said. "Can you believe our luck?"

They continued down the beach in this way—the beach was shorter now at high tide, closer to the palms and the small hotels and dance clubs and vendors selling barbecue chicken and pork on a stick. The smells of the food and the voices of the people wafted their way and slowly the lights of the castles were extinguished as the water flooded their rooms, their owners, the children, crying out in alarm, but laughing, enjoying the demolition of all their labors. For a moment, Stribley felt wildly carefree, felt as though he and Gemma were walking into a future that demanded nothing, not even that they pay attention. A wind kicked up and rustled the palms, and a fierce rain burst out of nothing, pounding the sand. Gemma screamed and covered her head, but Stribley continued to walk up the beach—he didn't want to stop until his pockets were empty.

"You missed that one," he shouted to Gemma and pointed to a spot beside a palm, the very one she had posed by earlier that afternoon. She gave him a curious look, as though she couldn't understand his language, then followed his finger to the dark shape of the palm, dancing madly in the wind. She dashed over to it, and as she reached down to pick up the shell, he shone his light on her. He saw through the screen of rain a look that he'd never forget, as though she saw in him something wonderful, something he had never before recognized, as though he, too, were small and delicate, something that could hold in its chambers all possibility and hope.

Sometimes in life, things simply happen that aren't really our fault, more like a force of nature. Stribley was in the middle of telling himself this excuse when the palm tree fell with the suddenness of a cartoon catastrophe. No warning, but a rustling of leaves and a shower of water and sand as it struck Gemma across the back. She didn't make a sound, and for a moment, he simply stood regarding her lying beneath the trunk of the tree. Palm leaves half-covered her. She had been pushed into the wet sand and she was hardly visible beneath the tree trunk, the base of which angled across her back, nearly obscuring her. He cried out and saw some curious boys slowly making their way over to Gemma as though confronting a wild animal.

What flashed in Gemma's mind, he'd never know. What flashed in his wasn't Gemma's life, but his own. He saw a future in which all his faults were suddenly and permanently crystal clear to everyone. It's one thing to have an anonymous affair while on vacation, but unless he simply walked away down the beach right now and pretended he had never had anything to do with Gemma, he imagined a certain spotlight would be cast on him as a foreigner. Maybe the police would try to shake him down, claiming he'd planned it. Maybe they'd take away his passport, prevent him from leaving the country. The story would appear in all the newspapers, maybe even make the international wire services. He imagined Rikki reading about this and expelling him from her heart, casting him irrevocably from her familiar orbit. He imagined E.K. reading about it and laughing. Before traveling to the Philippines, Stribley himself would have laughed had he encountered such a story, not out of cruelty, but with a sense of ironic detachment from the poor schmuck—a kind of prayer-laugh, that one's own life should not be reduced to such a stark punch line.

By now, a group of young men had gathered near Gemma, shouting instructions to one another, lights shining, alarmed voices sounding. "Be careful, be careful," Stribley heard someone yell as they began to lift the tree off and he made his way slowly down the beach, his lamp off but his head bent as though he were still scanning the beach for shells.

V

On the plane back home, seated by E.K., Stribley tried to sleep, not wanting to talk, but E.K. was in a jubilant mood.

"Can you believe it?" E.K. said, slapping Stribley on his leg.

"Yes," Stribley said and leaned towards the window.

"Can you *believe* it?" E.K. asked, sounding like a preacher.

"Yes," he said, shutting his eyes more tightly.

"Well, I can't believe it," E.K. said. "I'm rich. You know that? Mr. Ong has made me a very rich and happy man."

"I'm delighted for you both," Stribley said.

"And you, my boy, had a hand in it. You most certainly did, and for that, rich rewards await you, too. Rich rewards await my faithful flock."

Ahead of him lay almost twenty hours of travel, all that time to be in E.K.'s company and think before re-entering his life or some semblance of it. He tried to ignore E.K., but the man refused to be ignored. When he felt happy, he wanted everyone around him happy, too. E.K. wanted to know what he'd done with his spare time. They hadn't met up until a few hours earlier at the hotel, where Stribley had hurriedly packed after returning from Boracay. "Boracay?" E.K. had shouted into the phone the day before when Stribley called their Manila hotel on the off chance his boss would be there. "What are you doing in Boracay? Get your ass back to Manila. We're heading home tomorrow."

"You don't have to tell me what you were doing in Boracay," E.K. said now. "I can guess." He patted Stribley's leg again, this time gently. Stribley couldn't stand the thought of being comforted by E.K. "I know it's tough to leave them," he said. "It always is. I fall in love every day here. But it wouldn't have worked out. It never does. You have to watch yourself. After a while, you're looking at them over the breakfast table, wondering what in the world you can talk about. Nothing, that's what. You have nothing in common."

Stribley opened his eyes again. He couldn't fool himself; there would be no sleep for him on this flight. They had already passed the coast of Northern Luzon. Below, it was simply water, formless, the way the earth had been in the beginning, though somewhere down there he imagined low tide, some uninhabitable sandbar or atoll about to break the surface, its sand incomparably fine and white.

St. Charles Place

In those days, neither medical science nor therapy had advanced to the point where anyone knew what to do with my brother. My father wanted to take him out back and shoot him. We lived on a remote farm in upstate New York, and no one besides the doctor would have known. Yet, unenlightened as the time was, it was still not a time when doctors would countenance shooting a baby simply because he resembled, in every respect, a pig. Still, Father did not want us to grow too attached, and so he forbade us to name him. For the first five years of his life, I knew my brother simply as the Pig Baby.

His language, what he verbalized at least, consisted of grunts and snorts, though he needed no more to prove his intelligence. From an early age, he exhibited an interest and propensity for magic tricks. He started by pretending to capture my nose in his hoof or produce a penny from my ear, simple tricks, though sophisticated beyond his years.

Finally, when my brother was nearly six years old, Father relented and we were allowed to name him. I say "we" because it became a group decision, involving the energies of the eight of us: Mother, myself, and my other six siblings, for the better part of two weeks. Father wanted no part of the process, nor did my brother get involved. He neither knew nor suspected that he had finally been allowed to receive a Christian name, nor did he particularly seem to care.

Once you name an animal, there is no going back. You have made a contract with that animal to treat it humanely. As a rule, we do not name our cows Flossie, our pigs Arnold, or our chickens Betty for this reason. Life on the farm is no more brutal than life anywhere else, but the veneer over that brutality is not present as it is elsewhere. As a child, I remember a cow that partially delivered a stillborn calf. As it ran around the barnyard, the drooping calf half-emerged, we children tagged behind it, laughing joyously as we each took turns tugging at the dead calf, the winner the one who finally pulled it free. I don't remember who won, only the scene itself, nor do I remember if my brother was one of our laughing mob.

We named him Charles, after St. Charles Place in the game of Monopoly, a game my family loved. St. Charles Place, in the lore of my family, was a more coveted property than Boardwalk and Park Place combined, despite the fact that it is not a particularly coveted space on the board. But it had been the subject of a hotly contested all-night Monopoly binge one Winter's night when the property had switched hands time and again and eventually had decided the winner of the game, my father. Perhaps, in naming him thus, we had reached back with some kind of talismanic grace to a space in which Father could love this Pig Baby. I do not know. I only know that he did indeed accept and love Charles after we finally named him.

Charles was home-schooled as were we all. My father and mother belonged to a small religion the outside considered a cult because they did not understand us, and because of the relatively few members of the religion (there were less than a thousand at the time): The First Church of Common Sense and Good Manners. The beliefs were both straightforward and radical:

Mind your own business and no one will mind yours.
Stay away from people, places, and things that mean you harm.
Don't rely on the future but plan ahead.
Most of what you fear is in your own head, so get out of it
  once in a while.
You can't bring it with you, so don't try.
You can't go home again, so don't leave it.
Don't waste your time and don't waste the time of others.
Speak only when you have something useful to contribute.
Don't whine, complain, gossip, or indulge in self-pity and
  people will like you more.
There is such a thing as a free lunch, but usually it's someone
  else's lunch and you're the one treating.

We believed in a Creator, of course. But common sense dictated that, not having met the Creator, we had no personal knowledge of His/Her habits. And we didn't trust the accounts of others. We believed only what was in front of our faces. Most radically, there were no prophets of Common Sense and Good Manners. It was a religion wholly without divine revelation. Let other folks argue who was most favored by the Creator—we just wanted to be left to farm the harsh but lovely land where we made our homes. We weren't far from Palmyra, where the angel Moroni had appeared to Joseph Smith, but Smith had moved away. One could not live long in upstate New York and believe in much besides the simplest of answers to one's questions.

Which made much about Brother Charles problematic. Given the fact that most people mistook him for a pig, except for us, who upon reflection perhaps mistook him for human. Given the fact that Charles did magic tricks, or perhaps was magical and we simply mistook his magic for trickery. Given the fact that in our close-knit community, good manners and common sense were not supposed to conflict. A pig who, let's say, levitates on a regular basis would be considered an embarrassment rather than a miracle in our community, especially if one viewed him as not a pig and not a levitator, but a clever and strange boy with a physical defect. This was how we, his family were taught—by Father, by the tradition in which we had grown up. After all, we take most miracles for granted—electricity, film, and aviation to name a few, and even our explanations simply describe rather than truly explain. What I'm trying to say here is that if you grew up in an era of prophets, and your brother was Moses, your astonishment would be tempered by family secrets and the banalities of a shared history. Only now, years after the death of Charles, can I see him as outsiders do, and wonder whose view of him is correct. Charles was simply Charles to us, beloved in spite of his differences, not because of them.

The troubles surrounding Brother Charles began in his adolescence, when most troubles begin. He began to stray, quite literally. Nights, he would disappear from his room no matter how many locks we attached to the doorframe, accessible only from the outside, no matter how many bolts we screwed into the windows of his room. He somehow found his way out of his confinement without disturbing any of the locks or impediments we placed in his way. At first, we didn't know where he went and thought his nightly jaunts harmless (this was before we resorted to locks), but then reports started to filter back to us. A "demonic pig" appeared in the bedrooms of various members of our community, though our members did not believe in demons. Even at my young age, possessed of none of his talents or native intelligence, I could still discern in him a restless genius, and as he grew older, his demeanor became gloomier until he seemed a kind of Heathcliff on hoofs, absent a Catherine, the object of his malicious desire.

I remember the evening Constable Burnshaw brought home Brother Charles from one of his wanderings—Charles had traveled all the way to Potsdam, where he had disrupted the patrons of a diner by jumping on the tables and peeing on the meatloaf special. The Constable and my father huddled at the table, my mother standing anxiously over my father, one hand on his shoulder, the other hand stirring the pot of rendered fat from which she made our soap. Charles lay glassy-eyed at their feet, breathing raggedly every now and then. I remember thinking, why he's ill! Can't anyone see that? He's not in his right mind. The local Constable was a ruddy man whose vocation, hobby, and knack was tragedy. He picked up tragedy like fallen apples around a tree—that is the way trouble lies in our country. It's there for the picking. You only need to notice one trouble lying fallen among the many.

"I know you folks like to keep to yourselves," the Constable began.

"If we're treated well, we treat others well," Father said.

"Can't say I see it that way," the Constable said. "I'm going to have to ask you to rein in your . . . boy, before I have to do the reining. And there are damages, of course. And doctor bills."

"Doctor bills?" my mother asked anxiously. Charles gave a small snort. The Constable looked at him.

"Emmett Jorgensen. A case of nerves caused by the hubbub over at the diner. Caused by the doings of your . . . son."

"What do nerves cost these days?" Father asked.

"That's not for me to say," said the Constable. "But I don't want to hear a peep about your pig again."

"His name is Charles," said my father.

"Now look, Mr. Sayers."

"Now you look."

My father got up from the table and opened the screen door for the Constable, who left with a long face but no other words.

One evening not long after the visit from the Constable, Charles trotted up to me as I was chatting with our father. "Shall we play Monopoly, Brother and Father?" the voice in my head asked. Often I felt that Brother Charles was saying something to me, but I never spoke of this to anyone lest they think I was mad. In the Church of Common Sense, we certainly did not believe in mind reading, but we did believe in the Voice of Conscience and it was this voice I believed I mistook for Charles'.

My father and I regarded one another . . . expectantly, embarrassed.

"I was thinking . . .," my father said finally.

"Yes, let's," I said. "It's been a while."

Father retrieved the board from inside the toy chest in the alcove of our front hallway, where an antique telephone still hung, not used but workable. This was part of our ethic and aesthetic, too. The fact that something had outlived its usefulness did not make it useless, but simply different. We accepted objects as well as people for their differences, which made us a peaceable lot overall, and slow to anger.

"Mother," Father called.

"Sisters," I called. "It's time for Monopoly."

My older brothers were out in the fields, playing their rough games, so unlike Charles and myself.

The girls—Bessie, Tess, and Little Catherine—were in the kitchen, drawing and playing tiddlywinks by the potbelly stove, while Mother stood by, her brow sweating as she made soap, as she often did. But Monopoly had a magic effect on all of us, even her, and she took her cauldron of rendered fat off the stove and put the dripping ladle in the wash basin, wiped her gleaming face with her smock. "This time there will be no quarter asked for and none given," she said.

"You're the one who will be asking for mercy," Father said, and he laughed a fake, maniacal laugh.

He set up the board on the dining room table and we gathered around, Little Catherine and Tess already arguing over who would be the Banker. Each had hold of the money tray and pulled, and of course the tray slipped and Monopoly money tumbled to the floor.

"Girls!" Father said sternly. "Neither of you . . ."

Charles hopped up on the table and grabbed the board with his teeth and trotted out through his special entrance, like a doggie door, but bigger.

"Charles!" we yelled and followed him outside. We saw the boys walking toward us through the field, a brace of grouse between them, but then the field was gone—replaced by a brick street. On either side of the street stood stately houses with wide lawns where the barn and the orchard had stood before. At the entrance to the street, a hundred paces from the front door of our home, two large columns rose on either side. A pattern of bricks formed the words "St. Charles Place."

I have read that when the first Spanish explorer happened across the Grand Canyon, he barely made mention of it. When James Cook sailed into Botany Bay in Australia in 1770, the aboriginals on the shore seemed not even to notice the giant ship looming not so far off, precisely because in both cases, there was no context for the experience. The mind didn't know where to place such extraordinary sights and so it placed them nowhere. Imagine all the remarkable things we probably see and then reject because they shock our systems so profoundly as to produce no reaction at all. We seem unfazed because our minds have retreated into a safe room behind steel doors. So it was with the slice of Atlantic City, circa 1933, that appeared that crisp fall day in our backyard.

We did not wander the stately homes. We did not open doors and shout halloos into empty rooms. We did not wait for dark to see if the street lamps switched on. We did not call our relatives or friends on the old phone in the alcove. We greeted my brothers with warm shouts and congratulated them on their marksmanship, and they gave the grouse to my mother to clean. Then we turned around and entered the house again. The only sign that my family was flustered was my brothers' carelessness with their firearms. Had they been using common sense they would have immediately locked them up in the gun cabinet, but they simply leaned their guns by the front door, something they never would have done had they been themselves.

"Perhaps we could play a game of Go Fish," my father suggested.

"That sounds nice," said Tess.

"I agwee," said Little Catherine as though she had never argued with Tess in her life, and the eight of us settled down to a long game of Go Fish while mother cleaned the grouse.

None of us mentioned Charles or what had replaced our peaceful farm.

Ultimately, there is no shelter in life. Neither family, friends, nor the love of a close-knit community can protect us from ourselves or one another, and the same was true of Charles. What is it in people that makes them reject the notion of ambiguity?

Charles staggered in the next afternoon as if from an all-night drunk and collapsed by the fire in the living room. None of us spoke and he said nothing to us but lay breathing heavily by the hearth. He looked so alone and I wanted to comfort him but for the first time in my life, he seemed somehow frightening. None of us had yet gone outside to view the world as he had remade it, though he looked at us with beseeching eyes, as though we were missing something of great importance by not going outside. Perhaps he simply wanted to make us proud, but we could barely look at him.

Our mother gave him some of the leftover grouse she had cooked the night before, but he only stared at the plate.

"Whatever you've done, Charles," Father said, stroking his snout, "it doesn't change the fact that we will always treat you with the greatest courtesy as we have been taught by our Elders. We won't pry and ask you about anything you might not want to share. If you are cold, we will give you warm soup. If you are barefoot, we will lend you the money to buy sensible shoes at a thrift store. If you lack a ride, we will give you a lift. If you lack soap, we will make soap. If you are heartbroken, we will tell you you're better off without her. If you are worried, we will remind you that worry is wasted energy."

"Leave me alone," I heard Brother Charles say in my head. "You're speaking nonsense."

"Nonsense?" Father said. "It's common sense."

Father looked at us all with wide-eyed panic and withdrew his hand as though Charles had bit it. He had done the unthinkable and acknowledged the voice in his head as real.

Then Charles bit Father's hand.

"Damn you, Pig!" Father shouted and leapt to his feet. Charles rose to his feet, too, and then rose past his feet, by which I mean he levitated, and flew through the door.

By this time, we were all crying except for Father. "How do you explain that, Father?" I screamed, for the first time I could remember, raising my voice against his authority.

"I don't need to explain anything," he said with a calm that was almost unearthly.

I flung open the door. Had I been strong enough I would have grabbed Father and wrestled him by the neck under my arm and if I hadn't choked the life from him first, I would have brought him to the door and shown him St. Charles Place. I would have made him walk along the street with me. I would have brought him to the door of each stately home and walked inside. I would have brought him to each room, would have made him sit in the chairs, on the divans, would have clipped roses from the back-yard and made him cut his finger on a thorn.

But I was not that strong and what I saw when I opened the door was Brother Charles, trotting down the street, squealing. And then I saw Constable Burnshaw in pursuit and I heard the Constable shout for Charles to stop.

"No!" I yelled.

The Constable stopped his pursuit and took aim with great care. And then I heard the shot so close to my ear I dropped to the ground. And so did the Constable, as easy as a grouse.

Later, of course, came the shoot-out with the federal agents. I won't go into the heartbreaking details because we know the end results. Father and two of my brothers, and poor, innocent Little Catherine all perished in the conflagration. Our house burned to the ground as did most of St. Charles Place, except of course for the famous pillars which still bear the name of the fabled street.

We never saw Charles again. I believe he's dead, though the pilgrims who come to the ruins of our farm believe otherwise, that he's out there somewhere in the North Country, living off the land. They call him St. Charles. I have visited the farm once or twice over the years, have brought my tent and a sleeping bag right up against the hurricane fence the Feds erected around the ruined compound. I have glimpsed the pillars through the fence and have fallen asleep with the scent of the flower wreaths the pilgrims bring, and it brings me some solace. Once, I awoke in the middle of the night to the sound of a far-off loon. I went outside my tent and looked through the fence once again as if I might spy him there, as if he might tell me one more thing, show me something remarkable. For instance: that the material world is an illusion. But I have not heard him and it's not.

The 19th Jew

At her meeting with the Associate Dean, Edith Margareten asked the administrator, a woman in her mid-forties, about the climate for Jews at Notre Dame. "Oh, it's fine," she said. "I'm Methodist myself."

"Ah," Edith said.

The woman flipped through the pages of a scrapbook-sized volume. Edith looked down at her lap and smoothed out her wool skirt, which she had bought specifically for the interview. It was gray with little flecks of brown, and itchy. The dress looked Catholic on the rack, but she regretted buying it now. She placed her hands on her knees and regarded the Associate Dean while the woman flipped. Edith could hardly keep her eyes open. The woman bored her and she'd slept terribly the night before. The Morris Inn on campus had the skinniest beds, as hard as palettes, designed so that no one could possibly sleep—or consider sinning in them. Over every door in her suite, where normally one might expect to see a smoke detector, a cross hung or a swooning Jesus, or a proud Mary. Edith had unpacked, humming, "Left a good job in the city, working for the man every night and day." But no smoke detectors.

"Yes, we have seventeen Jews on campus," the woman announced, pointing at a page somewhere toward the middle of this mysterious book.

"What's one more?" Edith said.

"Exactly," the woman said, lifting her hand, palm up, and giving Edith a wide-open expression devoid of irony.

"You really keep track?" Edith asked, but it wasn't meant to be a question. "In a book."

This seemed to catch the Associate Dean by surprise. She sat up straight in her chair and locked her eyes on Edith. Edith wondered if this woman had ever read one of her books, if she even read books anymore, if she knew who Edith was. Going into the interview, she had asked the English Department Chair, a Milton scholar named Dan Massey, what an Associate Dean was. The *real* Dean had been off-campus, and so they'd come up with this low-cal Methodist version. He'd leaned over conspiratorially and whispered, "A mouse studying to become a rat."

"There might be more," the woman said.

"These are the ones you know of," Edith said.

The woman closed her scrapbook. "This is a Catholic institution, and part of our mission is to provide an exceptional education within a Catholic framework. But Notre Dame is known for its ecumenical atmosphere. The Catholic faculty hovers around 51 percent."

Edith smiled. "They hover, too." There was no possibility, she decided, of ever working for such a place. They probably wanted to hold the line, in any case, at seventeen Jews.

The job she had applied for—they had approached her, actually—was hardly a job at all, more like a sinecure: The Leo L. Ward Chair in Creative Writing. Edith, if she was offered the job and took it, would be its first recipient, and she was made to understand she could keep the job as long as she wanted. Father Ward had been head of the English Department in the '40s at Notre Dame, and had died in the early '50s—a volume of short stories, *Men in The Field,* was published posthumously with the Notre Dame Press. Edith had run across the book by chance at Gotham Book Mart, bought the copy, and read through it before her interview. But when she mentioned her find to the Chair of the English Department at a party in her honor, he cut her off. "Oh please," he squealed. "Don't embarrass me. *Men in the Field.* What, there were no women around?" Dan Massey made a gibbon-like face at her—all chin and eyes—pathetic, needy, and curious, and then he gave her a wide smile.

"I found some of the stories touching," she said. "But they're vignettes really. I wouldn't call them stories."

Dan Massey began to sputter and then broke into a kind of braying. Edith stood back and regarded him with a glass of white wine in her hand. No one at Notre Dame, she assumed, had even read Father Ward's stories in decades. They simply needed his name, the tradition he supposedly represented.

"Have you read them?" she asked.

"Oh please," he said with a wave. "*Men in the Field.*"

Dan Massey bent toward her and said, "Edith, we're lantsmen. I'm one-sixteenth Jewish. My great-grandfather." He bobbed in her direction—she couldn't say whether he was purposely making fun of a religious Jew benching, or if it was merely an effect of the wine. And he brayed as though this were an impressive revelation and not an insult, as Edith saw it.

"One-sixteenth," she said. "Coelum non animam mutant qui trans mare currant."

He smiled broadly at her.

"It's Horace," she said. "It means, 'Those who cross the sea, change the sky above them but not their souls.'"

"That's true," he said. "I know this sounds silly," and he bent close to her again with his gibbon expression. "but sometimes I feel my soul is Jewish. Especially when I read Singer."

She took a sip of wine and scratched her leg where the wool of her skirt had irritated it. The sea he had crossed was the shallowest body of water, and one hardly needed a ship, merely hip waders. Dan Massey was a fool. She was partial to fools. She wrote about them. She had married and divorced one. But this kind of fool, the academic variety, was not to her liking—his calibrations were slightly off.

She kept her demeanor cool but pleasant in a superior way, though the interview was over for her. Dan Massey was yet another reason she would never come to work for Notre Dame.

A week later, Massey called. He asked how much it would take to bring her. She didn't want to go, and she assumed that would be the end of it when she named an outrageous sum. The Chair paused and said, "Edith, you charmed everyone who met you."

Years later she still wondered on occasion what had charmed them so. In her circle of friends and enemies she was considered many things: pathologically self-obsessed, pedantic, and paranoid—not qualities one normally associated with charm. She had been ready to flatly refuse Massey's offer, despite the salary, but this revelation that they'd found her charming surprised her, weakened her resolve, lulled her into a kind of curious stupor that made her willing to suspend her natural suspicion of others.

"Really?" she said.

"Everyone's been talking about you. The graduate students, the members of the department. I've never seen such overwhelming support."

The week after the interview she'd spent denigrating the place to her friends and her relatives, so when she changed her mind, many were shocked. One friend said, "You can't leave New York. You'll die," as though New York were a rare blood type. Another asked if she'd have trouble finding fresh coffee. One friend placed South Bend in Wisconsin rather than Indiana and when Edith corrected him, he said, "I'm never *going* there." But the only reaction that truly angered her was her Aunt Judy's, a bitter and opinionated woman who had never approved of a decision of anybody's in her life. "Five years from now you'll have lost your voice," she said, "You'll be writing Willa Cather novels."

"My values are my values," Edith said.

"But you told me—they have Jesus on the side of the library."

Yes, he loomed over campus like a benevolent version of Godzilla over Tokyo, but even that didn't change her mind. She was ready for a change. And getting used to something like a hundred-foot Christ, being adaptable—that was part of living.

Seven years later, Edith was still settling into the place, but settling in comfortably. Edith's job made few demands on her—she lived in Chicago and commuted twice a week on the South Shore Railroad to South Bend, took a cab to campus, and kept an office hour. Usually, she had no interruptions and wrote during this hour—students didn't bother her because she didn't post her office hour or tell the departmental secretaries when it was. She didn't feel obligated to speak with any students who lacked the perseverance to track her down. Twice a year she taught a class to twelve hand-picked graduate students. Rather than discuss their work, she thought it more beneficial for them to hear about her own creative process—sometimes she asked them to write in class, and she took this opportunity to write as well. Sometimes she allowed them to read what they had composed.

Mostly, people left her alone. The Associate Dean had been right, after all, about the climate.

Before coming to Notre Dame, Edith had been spoken of as someone on the Nobel Committee's short list, and the list seemed to be getting shorter every year. She had been compared to everyone, and so believed, or hoped at least, that she really must be like no one: twenty-four reviewers had, over the course of her career, compared her to Paley, sixteen to Singer (for whom, they dutifully noted, she had translated), fourteen to Elkin, seven to Kafka, eleven to Malamud, three to Ozick, two to Bellow, and one lost soul had compared her to all seven. Most often, she was lumped with other Jewish writers, but sometimes Catholics, too. She dealt with moral issues in her work, with hypocrisy and comeuppance at the forefront—she often gave her characters Old Testament-type tests. They made mistakes, made the wrong decisions, like Jonah or Abraham, and that's why the Catholics liked her, she decided. They too were always making the wrong decisions: the Inquisition, their treatment of Native peoples in the New World, St. Domenic's eradication of the Albigensians on the orders of Pope Innocent the Third.

There was a man in her stories who almost always appeared, a fool named Brennerman, neither a Singer fool nor a Sholom Aleichem fool, a blessed know-nothing—nor a Shakespearean fool, wise but sad, a teaser. More of a trickster. Sometimes Brennerman knew a lot, sometimes he knew nothing. Sometimes he taunted her main character, Edith's alter ego, Francine Riemer. Brennerman liked to sit on Francine's shoulder like a conscience. Brennerman appeared in Francine's dreams, and Edith's too, told her to stop taking herself so seriously, that the world could live without her. Brennerman existed for Edith and Francine both in the world of their imagination and in the real world. He was based on a man Edith had once seen painting directional arrows in the lanes of the parking lot of the Green Acres shopping mall in Valley Stream, Long Island. She was there shopping with her mother, who lived in nearby Woodmere. The man's fellow workers were standing around smoking and talking while he was doing all the work. The lane which he painted was blocked off with orange cones. In the other lanes, all with freshly painted arrows, none of the cars paid any attention to the new directions. The man ignored the chaos around him just as the world ignored him. She decided this man's name was Brennerman. She never saw him again, but Edith's character, Francine, saw him all the time.

The names of God, Francine Riemer suspected, were legion, more than the combined last names of all of humanity, but how many more? How many last names could there be in the world? Had anyone counted, done a study, because she kept hearing new ones—Sloyer, Ege, Cashio, Paykue, Spawr. Francine wanted to know. She collected last names, from personal encounters, from far-off reports and news dispatches. She was a smart woman and knew, of course, that collecting names was an odd pursuit. She held out no hope for monetary gain. Her names had none of the intrinsic value of her mother's autograph collection—a Fred Astaire, a Tyrone Power, a Franchot Tone—nor of her cousin Sophie's collection of Italian leather decanters.

Francine's mother said this was an unhealthy occupation

—Preoccupation, Mother.

—Aren't you happy with your name?

—I'm happy with my name.

—Because if you're not happy, you should change it.

—I like my name, Ma.

—A name like Smith, perhaps. Or Jones. Or Arnold.
 That has a nice ring. Benedict Arnold.

—Ma!

—Eh, what does a pig know about noodles?

That was her mother's favorite saying. She used it all the time, but always, Francine thought, slightly out of context, and so Francine never really felt she understood what the saying meant.

Francine didn't feel unhealthy. Her dedication to names didn't interfere with her personal life (she had none), nor her work at the food co-op. But lately, she couldn't pass a man, a woman, a child on the street without desiring to discover who they were—at least as much as one can discover through the porthole of a last name.

In fact, when Francine and her mother were having this discussion, the one recorded nearly verbatim above, they were walking through the parking lot of a nearly famous suburban shopping mall, on a mission to buy a hat for Francine's mother, a belated—as always—birthday gift from Francine, when Francine and her mother walked by a man working in one of the lanes of the parking lot. The man, a young lanky fellow in overalls, a yarmulke perched on his head, was intently painting an arrow in the middle of the lane while three other workers stood above him, smoking and spitting and laughing, but not lending a hand at all.

The man's last name pierced Francine's foot like a shard of glass and made its way through her intestines to her heart. The name rose in her like a complaint. "Brennerman!" she shouted.

The men stopped laughing. Francine's mother stood still. The man painting the arrows looked up at her and smiled, an extraordinary smile, his top bicuspids missing, as though he'd actually given his eyeteeth, as the saying goes, but for what, Francine couldn't guess.

That was how the world was introduced to Brennerman and Francine Riemer. Brennerman had been gold to her. She owed him her entire writing career. But sometimes she still wondered, despite her success, where the source was of that internal voice, the one that made her stories possible. Sometimes she worried that she might be falling into a pernicious pattern, a diction that wasn't naturally hers, but wholly derivative. She worried even about Brennerman, her beloved fool, whether he was truly hers or not, whether she could rightfully claim him. She worried that what she presented to the world might not be true enough, but merely a caricature of Jewish literature. She despised the current crop of Southern writers for this reason—they often sounded so similar, she wondered whether they simply passed around a pad of paper to be continued where the last one left off. Perhaps the Nobel Committee discerned this same affliction in her own writing.

She did not want to be an imitator—discernible yes, within a tradition, but original enough so that she could not be typed or ethnically patronized. The comparisons people made between her and other Jewish writers bothered her less because she knew such comparisons were ultimately meaningless. Not only had she been compared to other Jewish writers, but often, she was compared to gentiles: Catholics—Flannery O'Connor, Graham Greene. Latin Americans—Cortázar, Márquez, Fuentes, Borges. Once when she'd written a book from a teenager's perspective, she'd been compared to Salinger and Harper Lee both. People needed to believe in such a great Literary Chain of Being, and that's why they made such comparisons.

Singer, perhaps, was to blame for her insecurities. He had fed them, been quite cruel to her. She had known Singer well, had translated some of his early stories when she had worked at Noonday Press and later at Farrar, Straus as a young woman in the '50s and '60s. In later years, she lost touch with him, partly because of Singer's secretary, Joanne, who treated him like a wind-up toy. The world treated him much the same, a little Yiddish gnome, reduced, catalogued, purchased. All of his well-cultivated eccentricities, the parakeets in his home that perched on his head, his vegetarianism, the requisite copy of the *Daily Forward* under his arm, were part of the package, accessories one might purchase for a Barbie doll.

She had been deceived by that version of the man when she first met him, but saw another side once when she had dinner at his apartment. They had been working on a translation of one of his stories, although to call her work translating was a misnomer. Her knowledge of Yiddish was limited to a few curses her uncle Al had taught her. Singer did the rough translations himself and his translators polished his prose. They had been working on one of the stories from *Gimpel the Fool* all day, when Singer suggested she stay for dinner. When his wife walked in the door after work—she worked in the women's sportswear department at Saks—he ordered her to prepare dinner for them both, and then all through the meal he ignored her. Edith and Singer had been discussing the Suez Canal, and when his wife offered her opinion, he paid no attention, except to tell Edith pointedly that it was nice, for once, to have an intelligent conversation with an intelligent woman.

Edith had a hard time forgiving herself for being so young and stupid. She had showed him a story, but only because he had asked to see it. This was after they slept together one afternoon not long after the dinner with his wife. That night, she had a nightmare that Singer told her she was completely without talent, and when she woke up she was glad it was only a dream, but it turned out worse. He told her that he was astounded how poor her writing was. He had assumed she was good because Roger Straus had recommended her, but now he wasn't even sure she had the ear to help him with the polishing of his own roughs.

"Do you want me to leave, Mr. Singer?" she had asked.

"What does your mother do?" he asked her.

"My mother?" she said, wondering whether he wanted her mother to translate, to sleep with him, too. "My mother sells hats."

"That's a good occupation. You should sell hats, too. Forget writing. It's a tough business."

Sometimes, in her dreams, she still heard herself asking meekly, in her craven voice, "Do you want me to leave, Mr. Singer?"— and waiting for his reply. He just looked at her with that impish smile. "Hats. I'll say it again. Sell hats."

Edith was asked to serve on a committee—an unusual occurrence, the first, actually, of its kind. She was not expected under normal circumstances to serve on committees, nor to attend department meetings—though she had, on occasion, been prevailed upon to serve on the thesis committee of a particularly promising graduate student or two. But this committee was different. It was a university-wide committee established to decide on an award, a kind of junior version of her post, the Ernest Hoover Fellowship, named in honor of another beloved former professor and writer from the English Department. The award would be given annually to a young writer in early- to mid-career, and provide a stipend for the writer to finish a project of exceptional merit.

Dan Massey, who was no longer the Chair of English, but the new Associate Dean, assured her that her presence on the committee was crucial, that she was the only one on campus who had the knowledge, experience, and prestige to make such an important decision. "Anyway," he said. "You can't leave me alone. I'll be the only Jewish person on the committee."

"You're not a Jew, Dan," she said.

"Why don't you ever humor me, Edith? Hey, maybe you can make me an honorary Jew."

"That's a tall order."

"Who am I, trying to fool you?" he said and laughed.

She hated the man, but he seemed to think they were best friends. She knew he was right. They needed her on this committee, not because she was Jewish, of course, but because no one else could be trusted.

Edith spent much more time at the task of sorting though the applications than she had originally anticipated. Most of the writers who applied were clearly not competitive. To say that they were beginning writers would be to assume that they even knew where "go" was. A beginning predicted an end, but with most of the applicants, the only end Edith could envision was her own premature death, a kind of literary aneurysm. Other applicants were clearly unworthy because they were too far along in their careers. One such writer was one of those who had initially expressed such horror at the thought of her accepting the job at Notre Dame, at venturing outside of two hundred miles from New York. Now, he warmly addressed his application directly to Edith and ended his letter by writing, "I hear reports that you're getting along famously in Indiana, so it must be bearable. But I always thought you'd moved to Wisconsin!! What's the difference, right?" She gave him a handwritten reply.

DEAR BRUCE,

When I told you I was leaving New York for the Midwest,
you said that it didn't matter where South Bend was
because you were never going there. You were right.

After a month, she came across an application she liked, from
a Hispanic poet with the single name Mi. The poet was barely in
her thirties and had already won every fellowship in the known
universe and hardly needed another: the Hodder Fellowship,
the Stegner, a Whiting, a Guggenheim, an NEA. But it was difficult to deny the power of her poems. Mi had been an addict
and prostitute in Houston, and she wrote persona poems from
the points of view of other hookers and addicts, gang members,
white businessmen, cops. While those poems were good, there
was one *amazing* sequence of poems that threaded through Mi's
manuscript, a fanciful but searing series of prose poems in which
the world's past revolutionary leaders all visited Mi, and while
she tried to talk politics with them, all they wanted to do was to
satisfy their personal sexual urges. In one poem, she masturbated
Mao. In another, she had oral sex with Ho Chi Minh. She whipped
Lenin. She had straight sex with Che, while Fidel watched. All
of them, in their turn, made excuses for not paying her. The title
poem of the manuscript, "The Long March," detailed a night
in jail, trying to keep her head from exploding, as Mao, in the
form of a fly buzzing her, berated her for being caught, for having it easy, for betraying the others who hid in caves and evaded
planes, machine guns, torture, and bombs of the Japanese and
Kuomintang. The poem was an incredible meshing of Chinese

history against the backdrop of mini-mart America, and ended in a gorgeous and surprising stanza in which the poet revealed she was writing the poem from the Bellagio Center for the Arts in Italy, and that the fly lay dead on her windowsill.

Such a presence would knock their frocks off at Notre Dame.

At the next meeting of the committee, Edith suggested Mi for the fellowship. There were six members from various departments and disciplines, chaired by Dean Smoot, the former Associate Dean and sometime Methodist (who had since converted) who had interviewed Edith and allowed that one more Jew would not tarnish Notre Dame's Golden Dome. There was a moment of silence while the members passed around the folder, glanced at it to refresh their memories, and then looked at their laps, all except for Stan White-Watson, who agreed with Edith that Mi should be awarded the fellowship.

No one in the English Department, or anywhere, as far as Edith could tell, cared for him. But unlike her colleagues, Edith did not pretend to like him. His name was Stanford White-Watson, and as he was fond of telling people within three minutes of meeting them, he had been named after the famous architect Stanford White. Stan was an opportunist, a loudmouth, and a bully: one of those people who throws back his head and laughs after saying something terribly vituperative, but his jolliness counteracted his meanness, and so people rarely knew how to respond to him, except to laugh along in a kind of forced self-deprecation. When people spoke of powers within the university, Stan White-Watson was always among the first names mentioned. As far as Edith could tell, the source of Stan's power as well as his pretend popularity was his complete readiness and willingness to give a cocktail party at a moment's notice. When a candidate needed to be entertained or a visiting dignitary feted, Stan was the man with the wine and cheese and the full liquor cabinet.

The reason Stan and Edith did not get along had to do with a party given in Stan's honor. A couple of years earlier, Stan had left his wife of nineteen years and his two children, and had moved in with David Kitto from Political Science. Although Edith had not known Stan's wife, Clarise, well at all (nor anyone else at Notre Dame), the rest of the department had been friends with her—but the response by a number of them to the breakup of Stan's marriage was to hold a party for Stan to celebrate his coming out. None of this interested Edith in the least, and she had refused to go to the party, not because of his sexual orientation, but because she saw the breakup of his family as a tragedy, not a cause for celebration. She had told him as much when he asked her in the hall one day why she hadn't been there.

"Too bad I didn't know," Stan said. "Clarise was holding a concurrent party for self-righteous homophobes," and he threw his head back and started to shake with laughter.

"I think that what you did was selfish," she said. "But private nonetheless. It's the poor taste of your friends, nothing more, that kept me away from this party."

Edith had had enemies before—a natural result of her own honesty and unwillingness to compromise her values—but none seemed as contemptible and bilious as Stanford White-Watson. Now she found herself in an uncomfortable alliance with him.

"We would like to have a Hispanic," the Dean finally told them, "but not this Hispanic."

"What do you mean, you'd *like* to have a Hispanic?" said Stan.

"I have to agree with the Dean," said Jack Ormsby from Engineering. "Her poems seem pushy."

The Dean looked at Edith and smiled.

Another member of the committee, Millicent Kent from Copy Duplicating Services, mentioned that she had just noticed that the ad for the position had a comma splice in it that no one had caught.

"My God," said Massey, grabbing the ad and peering at it closely. "I can't believe that got by us."

He passed the piece of paper glumly to Dean Smoot. "Too late now," she said. "We'll have to watch that in the future. That does not reflect well on us."

"I want to talk about Mi," said Edith.

The committee members looked across the table at her. Stan White-Watson tapped the edge of the table with a pencil. "Do you always have to be the center of attention, Edith?"

"The poet," Edith said. "The Hispanic poet who, for some reason, threatens this committee."

"I'm surprised she doesn't threaten you, too," Stan White-Watson said in a nasty tone and laughed again, but Edith ignored him. "What exactly about her makes you so uncomfortable?" she asked the others.

"She's vulgar," said Millicent Kent.

"Tasteless," said the Dean.

"We just don't like her work," said Ormsby.

"I don't think you're judging her *work*," Edith said. "You're judging who you think she is. Judge the work."

"It's vulgar," said Millicent Kent.

"I don't get it," said Ormsby.

"This is making me ill," said Edith.

"Me, too," said Stan. "We should at least bring her to campus."

"We're not authorized to bring anyone to campus," said the Dean. "We make our decision and that's who wins the fellowship."

"Aren't we allowed to simply not like her work, to think she's not very good?" asked Millicent Kent.

"No," said Edith. "*You're* not." She stood up and pointed a finger at the woman, who shrank a bit in her seat. "What do you think, Dan?" she asked Massey.

Massey simply gave her a befuddled smile like the fool he was. But in the end, Edith and Stan prevailed, with the pliable support of Dan Massey.

There was a connection between this young poet's work and her own, Edith felt. They shared other things in common as well, such as a fear of flying. Mi currently had a Bunting Fellowship at Radcliffe, and so took the train from Boston to New York to Chicago. The committee didn't even have to ask Edith to pick her up at Union Station. Edith volunteered. She didn't want anyone getting to the young poet before she did, and possibly saying something off-putting.

On the cab ride from her Lake Shore Drive apartment to Union Station, Edith imagined a conversation between herself and Mi.

Edith was always composing, talking to herself, imagining outcomes. This was what made her such a fine writer, her deep interior life, the almost spiritual plane on which she hovered.

   —*It's an injustice that you have not won, says Mi.*
   —*I'm sure you'll win someday, says Edith. You've won
      everything else.*
   —*I'd tell them that they should have given it to you, just as
      Hemingway said that Isak Dinesen should have won—
      though she was a colonialist, hardly a better choice.*
   —*Out of Africa, indeed, says Edith.*
   —*Perhaps you threaten them, says Mi. You must.
      But I would take that as a compliment.*
   —*I do, child, says Edith.*

Edith, absorbed in her dialogue with Mi, didn't notice until the cab stopped that the cabbie had taken her to the Northwestern Station rather than Union Station. By the time she arrived at Union Station, she was twenty minutes late and was sure that for once a train had probably arrived on time.

In the huge waiting hall of Union Station, the indistinct echoes and cries like exotic birds bounced off the stone walls. The place sounded almost haunted. Noise permeated the waiting area, a wall of sound created by a thousand travelers. Edith sat on a bench and scanned the crowd for the poet. A chubby black girl sat beside Edith, patting out some insistent tune on her thighs, looking in every direction at once, chatting manically with her mother and sister. Edith looked at the girl's thighs, then directly at the girl, who seemed not even to notice Edith. Twenty years ago, Edith would have pretended to be color-blind, would have perhaps started up a conversation with the girl to prove to herself and anyone within earshot that she was color-blind. But she thought now, if I cast this girl in a story, would I mention she was black? Yes, this was the first thing she noticed about the girl. The second thing she noticed was the girl's weight, also a corporeal consideration. Why mention them? But what stood out for Edith in this hall of sound was that drumming the girl did on her thighs. Would Edith have noticed a thin white girl drumming on her thighs? She hoped so. It was the sound that annoyed her, only the sound, insistent and harsh.

Edith noticed a dark-skinned-but-not-black woman standing by a bank of phones, who seemed to be waiting for someone. The woman was tall and had an aquiline nose and a dancer's posture. Edith fled the thigh-pounding black girl and approached the young woman with a warm smile and extended hand.

"Are you Mi?" she asked the woman.

The woman looked briefly with alarm into Edith's eyes. "What?"

"You're not Mi, are you?" Edith said.

The woman seemed to notice something far above her and then off to the left.

Edith backed away. "Mi. It's her name. Mi. Mimi."

But the woman seemed not to be listening. She was frozen with a grim expression, almost fearful.

"Does she look like Mi?" a voice boomed behind her.

Edith turned and saw Mi. No one Edith had ever seen looked like Mi. Her hair was reddish-blond, not brown as in the picture Edith had seen, but as she drew close, Edith could see this was a wig. Mi's most striking aspect was not her reddish-blond wig, but the full-length black fur coat the poet wore, worth thousands of dollars, Edith was certain, but not the most appropriate fashion statement these days.

"She is not Mi. I am Mi."

"Edith Margareten," said Edith clearly and firmly to let Mi know just whom she had snapped at so imperiously. Edith held out her hand. The woman brushed her fingers to Edith's and drew them back as though Edith's fingers were sticky. She looked impassively at Edith, who panicked and thought, *She doesn't like my work. She thinks I'm bourgeois, pretentious. She'd better like my work.*

Mi hardly spoke a word to Edith until they got into the cab to go to the InterContinental on Michigan Avenue, where Mi was to spend her first night. She turned to Edith. "So, are you a writer?" Mi asked Edith the same way Edith asked teenagers at book signings who obviously wanted to be.

Edith suddenly felt tired, and could barely keep her eyes open. She wondered if Mi had been sent by a vengeful God to mock her, to humble her. She was Mi. Mi was she. It was a dirty trick, and she wouldn't succumb, not even to God.

"Books," Edith said. "Many books."

"Tell me their titles. I want to read them." But she did not sound convincing and Edith could barely find the energy to talk.

"*My Ántonia . . . Death Comes for the Archbishop,*" she whispered.

"What? Speak louder."

"My books are unimportant," Edith said.

Mi nodded. "There are so few books of true importance."

And then Mi started telling her about a trip she'd taken to the former Soviet Union a number of years back in which she gave a reading with Yevtushenko and Bob Dylan. "At the end of the reading, they gave me the flowers—they only give flowers to one person. The Russians love me." Then she launched into a tirade against the Academy of American Poets. "They continue obstinately to ignore me."

Edith nodded but she wasn't listening. She was thinking of a new story, and while she didn't know exactly what this one was going to be about, she saw the last image quite clearly. She saw Brennerman as a thief in this story, breaking into Francine's apartment and painting arrows on the walls of her kitchen. "What are you doing to my beautiful apartment?" she'd have Francine scream at Brennerman. "I thought this is what you wanted. Isn't this what you always wanted?" Brennerman would ask, and that would be the end of the story. Now she only needed a story to fit that ending.

The next day there was no one to meet Mi at her hotel to bring her to South Bend. Mi did not make it to Notre Dame, perhaps not even out of Chicago. Edith never found out what happened to Mi. No one told her and she did not ask. The other committee members were wise enough not to mention the word "Mi" in

Edith's presence, except as a personal pronoun. At the next meeting of the committee, Edith hardly said a word, and half-listened to their recommendations—until Massey brought up the name of William Cradle Flower.

"I don't remember William Cradle Flower," Edith said.

"We were holding it back from you," said Ormsby, the buffoon from Engineering, staring into his coffee cup, which had a replica of the mosaic Jesus on the side of the library. "We didn't want to excite you and Stanford too much."

The faculty received two free tickets to every Notre Dame football game, and ever since the committee had formed, she'd given her tickets to Ormsby. But no more. She'd go back to tossing them in the trash, maybe ripping them up with great ceremony and scattering them in the hallway. The only time she'd ever been near a Notre Dame football game was once when she went to observe the strange men who prayed at the grotto and lit candles before every home game. Ormsby was probably their head priest, their oracle.

"He's just kidding," Massey said. He smiled at Edith warmly, and for the first time, she felt a nickel of warmth for him, too. Maybe he wasn't hopeless.

Ormsby blew on his coffee. "The application came in late, past the deadline."

"Who cares?" said Edith. "Is he good?"

"He's written a novel," said Massey, "that takes place—"

"If you like that kind of thing," said Ormsby. "But it didn't go anywhere."

"It didn't have a car chase?" White-Watson asked.

"I think it's a beautiful novel," said Millicent Kent. "It's mythic."

Edith looked down at her notes, pursed her lips, and waited a few seconds. Then she looked up at the woman from Copy Duplicating Services and said, "The term 'myth' implies an ir-reality that native people do not feel. For them, there is no border between the empirical world and the world of dreams or myth. Ultimately, it's a patronizing term."

"Oh . . . well . . . what I meant was . . .," said Millicent Kent and she put on a long face. "I didn't mean to patronize. . . ."

"Are we allowed to ask his tribal affiliation?" Massey asked the Dean.

"Cradle Flower," said the Dean, picking at something on the sleeve of her jacket. "Cradle Flower. I can't stop saying it."

Edith took the novel home with her to Chicago, read half of it on the train, and finished it that night at her kitchen table while sipping tea. She finished it by two but didn't get to sleep until dawn—a combination of the tea and the excitement of discov-ering such a talent kept her from sleeping. The novel was titled *Incurable Hearts,* and that was the main character's name. Incur-able Heart was a Crow who, by day, worked as a park ranger at the Little Bighorn National Monument and by night as a blackjack dealer at the Little Bighorn Casino just outside of the battlefield. Incurable Heart felt conflicted about the past of his tribe because the Crow had scouted for Custer against the Sioux, their enemies, and had been rewarded with one of the largest reservations of all the tribes by the federal government. He hardly ever slept and had visions of a coyote spirit, a trickster who was always confusing him. Sleepless and befuddled, he sometimes dealt blackjack to the RV tourists at the monument who wanted to hear about what a hero Custer was, and who still referred to the battlefield as the Custer National Memorial. And sometimes Incurable Heart gave lectures on Benteen and why he wasn't able to come to Custer's aid, but he delivered these lectures at the casino while dealing to the same tourists who had visited the battlefield earlier in the day, the tourists who now wanted only to drink beer, sing karaoke in the lounge, and get rich. Eventually, he was fired for incompetence and set off on a kind of inverted Candide-like adventure, accompanied by Coyote, who, like Pangloss in *Candide,* had his own reductive and impossibly buoyant outlook, despite the many deprivations and injustices they encountered on the road. Finally, they wound up in Los Angeles at the La Brea Tar Pits, where Coyote fell in and was trapped forever among the mastodons, despite Incurable Heart's best efforts to save him by making a lifeline out of his Levi's 501s. The novel ended with Incurable Heart spending the night in the drunk tank, arrested for vagrancy, public intoxication, and indecent exposure, trying to convince anyone who would listen that's it wasn't too late to save his friend, that Coyote could hold his breath for an impossibly long time.

This was the new voice of a generation. Elements in his work reminded her of Márquez and Calvino, Kundera and Rushdie, Donald Barthelme and DeLillo, Erdrich and Morrison, Malcolm

Lowry. But of all the work that his could be compared to, William Cradle Flower's felt most like her own vision. She gleaned in his work a brilliance that she rarely saw in any of the younger writers. And best of all, unlike Mi, William Cradle Flower had not been discovered by anyone else.

The host of the welcome party for William Cradle Flower was Stan White-Watson. No surprise there.

He lived in a sprawling house on Riverside Drive built in the Knute Rockne days. It wasn't much of a river. Not the Hudson, but the St. Joseph. And not New Jersey on the other side but . . . the other side. After all these years, she still missed New York, and secretly felt sometimes that she'd made the wrong decision to come to the Midwest. Her reputation, while still solid, seemed to be stagnating, and she worried that people back east had forgotten her. Here, a party was only a party. People were supposed to have fun—they could do no more. Not that she missed the people, but the parties she used to attend back east were more than gatherings of people, but gatherings of reputations. The people took up only part of the space—their reputations filled the gaps.

William Cradle Flower, who was being escorted by Dan Massey, had not yet arrived when Edith showed, but half of Notre Dame seemed to be there, including many from her own department whom she had never met or whose names she'd forgotten. She burrowed through them, found her way to the dining room, and poured a glass of wine from the many bottles on the table. Retreating to a corner, she stood there with her coat still on and sipped, glancing away when anyone looked in her direction.

"It's the Phantom," Stan said, reaching out his arm toward her in mock horror.

The people gathered around him turned and smiled meekly at her. "Edith," said Howard Salinas, the new Chair of the Department, waving her over, obviously trying to counter Stan's rudeness. Stan, Edith knew, acquired his personality via his liquor stock, and most of it was pretty cheap—so she rarely was offended anymore by his barbs.

"Stan was just telling us about something called 'Soul Retrieval.'"

"At a place called the College of Shamanistic Healing in Santa Fe," said Tess Narokin, Howard Salinas' wife, who taught Russian and French.

"Make fun of it if you like," said Stan, "but I found it healing. We all need to be healed. All of us."

He looked at Edith, but she said nothing and simply took a sip of her wine. She felt as though they were setting her up—Stan, especially, seemed on edge, already drunk.

"I, for one, prefer not to be healed," she said finally.

"What do you mean?" asked Tess.

"I mean that I'm a kind of Christian Scientist of the spirit. I acknowledge the sickness in my soul, but refuse all known treatment, especially from Doctors of Divinity."

"I knew she'd make fun of me," said Stan.

"I'm serious," she said. "My refusal to be treated makes me a better writer."

The front door opened, and Dan Massey appeared, accompanied by a wisp of a man dressed in jeans, a sport jacket, a blood-red shirt, and little rope tie. He stood there for a second looking as though he'd entered the wrong bathroom and wanted to turn around, but Dan Massey ushered him in and closed the door. Stan, of course, was the first to greet William Cradle Flower. "Stanford White-Watson," he said solemnly, grasping William Cradle Flower's hand, and leading him into the living room. "One of those three-barreled names like yours," he said, but Edith cut him off before he could launch into the extended history of his name. She could almost hear his teeth grinding. If there was one way to torture Stan White-Watson, it was to cut him off, either speech-wise or liquor-wise. Like so many of these academics, he had a compulsion to hear himself speak.

"Edith Margareten," she said, extending her hand. "Your novel was superb. Welcome."

William Cradle Flower looked at her with wide little-boy eyes. But he wasn't a little boy. His hair was thinning and he had deep smile lines around his mouth. His eyes were blue and his hair was sandy blond, what Edith's mother had always called dirty blond.

"Can I get you anything to drink?" Stan asked.

"A rum and Coke," said William Cradle Flower.

"Rum and Coke?" said Stan. "How old *are* you?" and he gave one of his trademark laughs and left.

Massey, standing in between Edith and William Cradle Flower, glowed like he was marrying them.

"We had dinner at the LaSalle Grill," Massey told Edith. "Bill was telling me that he admires your work more than almost anyone alive." Massey was speaking loudly, distinctly, and a little more slowly than normal.

"Do you like to be called 'William' or 'Bill'?" Edith asked, wishing she could protect this frail and quiet young man from the buffoons around them.

He seemed not to hear her. He brought a finger up to his mouth and started gnawing at a fingernail.

"Here's your rum and Coke," Stan said, handing the drink to Cradle Flower. "So, as I was saying, my father was a frustrated architect, and he named me after Stanford White. I suppose he would have preferred that I become an architect, too, but all I build are castles in the air. My last name is Watson, like Sherlock Holmes' assistant. But I'm not a doctor, though I have a doctorate, and the detective I assist is not Mr. Sherlock Holmes, but Mr. Jacques Derrida. The crimes we investigate are crimes of hermeneutics."

William Cradle Flower looked up as though a smoke alarm had gone off. His eyes brightened, glowed almost mischievously, and he said, "My father was a frustrated rabbi."

"He wanted to be a rabbi?" Edith asked.

"He was a rabbi . . . he was frustrated," said Cradle Flower. "For a while, I wanted to be a rabbi, too. But I have always felt, even as a little boy, like an Indian."

Edith's stomach turned over. She rooted in her coat for a hard candy. She was down to her last one. The little candy sat snugly in its roll, a long snake of wrapping trailing around it.

The novel was good, she thought, but not that good. If she hadn't been so tired when she read it, she would have discerned how derivative it truly was.

"We have met before," said Cradle Flower to Edith.

"Oh boy," she said. "When was that?"

"2,300 years ago, when I was a Levite. That was before the Temple was destroyed." He pointed to Massey. "You made music." He pointed to Stan. "You made the fire."

"What did she do?" Stan asked, indicating Edith.

"You made the sacrifice," Cradle Flower said, turning to her.

For a second, Edith could see herself with the knife in her hand, poised over the animal's throat.

"But those other people no longer exist. We have all changed our names. I had my name changed to fit my true nature. I am a Miami warrior. I was here in South Bend when LaSalle came through. I sat under the Council Oak and exchanged gifts with him."

Cradle Flower gulped down his rum and Coke and sat beside Edith on the Victorian love seat she occupied. He smiled shyly at Edith and said in an almost-normal voice, "I'm so happy you liked my writing."

Edith popped up and the candy went down her throat undissolved.

"What was your name before you changed it?" she asked. She wondered what the Dean would put in her scrapbook under Cradle Flower's name. "In this lifetime."

"As ego fades, we return to the elements that surround us," Cradle Flower said.

"Your name," she said again. "Your real . . . name."

"Ha ha ha," Cradle Flower sang in a singsong. "Who's afraid? Ha ha ha. Who's afraid?" and he rocked back and forth in the love seat, his eyes fixed on Edith.

"This man is insane," said Edith to Massey. "We can't award him anything."

Massey fluttered his hand. "Legally, I don't know," he said. "It's done, Edith. And it's only for a year."

"But, our reputations," Edith said weakly. She saw herself in a cemetery, dressed in mourning. She saw herself rending her garments. She saw Mr. Singer. "I told you," he said. "Hats . . . are your true calling."

She bent down and pulled one of the large buttons off Cradle Flower's red shirt like an officer stripping a subordinate of rank. "We paid for an Indian."

"Edith," said Massey.

"I always knew she was a bigot," Stan said, and gave one sharp laugh. "A hell of a nom de plume," he said to Cradle Flower. "You had us fooled. Oh well." Stan looked at Massey and said, "You need your drink freshened?"

Cradle Flower stood up and stopped his singsong. He stood stiffly at attention, his eyes on some invisible point like a national flag that only he could see, but which claimed his undying loyalty. "My name," he shouted, "My undying name . . ."

The room quieted and they waited for the man who called himself Cradle Flower to speak. Even Edith waited, as though an eternal mystery were about to be solved.

"My one true name is Crevecoeur," he said.

"Heartbreak," yelled Tess Narokin with the intensity of a jackpot winner. "That means heartbreak in French."

"Or Willow," said Cradle Flower. "Or Otter . . . Mackinaw Island . . . Space Needle . . . Or the wind. Or Grandfather. Or The Spirit That Resides in All Things, or Bebe Rebozo, Jack Lord."

"You never know," said Stan, draining his glass.

"It's still a hell of a novel," said Massey.

"Or Dream Pillow," Cradle Flower said. "Skunk Medicine. Or the Owl. The Pussycat. At sea in a pea green boat. We are living in the time of the Seventh Fire. We have no need for names."

Edith wanted to cry, wanted to jump into the St. Joseph. Arrows. Everywhere, she saw arrows. In their hands, instead of drinks, through their hearts, on the walls. On the floor. Like a goofy joke, she imagined an arrow poking through her head. This is what she looked like, what she'd been carrying around for so many years, the source of her pain, her voice, everything rich and bankrupt, ridiculous and blessed.

"What a fool," she said to no one in particular, patting the side of her head. She looked around the room and saw her lantsmen, her people. She was almost ready to embrace them.

"Brennerman," she said, a name she detested now.

"Or Brennerman," the man said, nodding, his eyes no longer lucid.

The List

To Our Friends,

Sam and I had an eventful year, and while we would like to correspond with each and every one of you to wish you a joyous holiday, time won't allow it, so we hope you won't mind this form.

Corrine, our youngest, sparkled in her dance school's performance of *Swan Lake*. Though she stubbed her toe on one of the stage lights, and broke it (the toe, not the light), she struggled on like the little trouper she is without telling anyone—even after the show was over, she refused to tell anyone. Sam thinks I push her too hard and that she is afraid to admit her failures to me, but I think that, in fact, she has inherited some of Sam's Midwestern stoicism, and thinks that to admit pain is sinful. I personally couldn't care less about my children's failures. All I ask is that they do their best, and then I stand back and beam.

For whatever reason, Corrine didn't tell either of us about her broken toe until weeks later when the toe became infected and then gangrenous. By that time, it was too late and the foot had to be amputated.

Corrine has adapted well, as have I, but Sam—out of grief, I suppose, or simply as an excuse—started having an affair with one of his students. He thought that I didn't suspect, but actually, I couldn't have cared less. I think only the siege of Leningrad lasted longer than the amount of time it's been since we made love. I'm not trying to gain your sympathy here because, in truth, I'm as much to blame for the dissipation of our marriage as Sam—his stoicism, my denial, we're a tag team of dysfunction. But we've made it twenty years together, and we send out almost two hundred Christmas cards a year, the picture on the front of our loving family in front of the Christmas tree virtually the same but for Sam's hairline and my more and more insistent smile, the children a few inches taller, the tinsel shiny as always. I'm not trying to depress you. Really. There's nothing I'd like more to tell you than that we're completely fulfilled, as I'm sure you'd like to tell us. To admit anything less is to admit defeat, even a kind of moral failure. Happiness has become, not an inalienable right to be sought, but a duty, and if we fail, we risk censure, we risk being taken off the list. When Gretchen Sanders went into rehab, she was taken off the list. When Harrison Elders was indicted, when Jeanine Watanabe . . .

The fact is, I don't really care about any of you, or at least I care as little about you as you care for me. This shouldn't shock any of you, not really. If you really cared about me and Sam,

wouldn't you do more than reserve one stamp a year to send
me a list of all your petty triumphs and comic mishaps? Is
that friendship? Why do we keep doing it? I suppose we want,
ultimately, to believe in those telephone commercials that try
to convince us that we're all intimately connected somehow,
though in fact we're thousands of miles apart, and if one or the
other died tomorrow, we would grieve for a short time, think of
the last time we spoke or saw one another, and then scratch the
name off the list. One less stamp.

What does it mean to you to receive this letter year after year
from me? I suppose I'm breaking some law by writing the truth
to you. How do you picture me now? With a gun in my hand,
my husband and his grad student nearby? Or drunk, sitting
alone with the gun stuck to my temple? Or in the garage, the
door closed, the motor running?

Don't be so melodramatic. Perhaps, if you receive this letter,
you'll call me up, and you'll say, "Jean, I didn't know, what's
going on? You sound so desperate." You'll say to your spouse or
your cat or the mirror, "It's obviously a cry for help," and you'll
see yourself as my rescuer. Or maybe you won't. Maybe you'll
not even have read this far, past the greeting. After all, I don't
read your letters either. I just look at the picture and shake my
head and say, "Wow, those kids are growing." So maybe for
the past twenty years, you've been sending me cries for help
disguised as holiday greetings, and I've been just as callous as I
imagine you to be.

The truth is, nature concocted a more brutal revenge on Sam
than ever I would have been capable or would have wished

on him. Quite out of the blue, he developed a rare disease that makes the skin leathery and reptilian and then cracks and bursts into ulcerous lesions. This disease is terrifyingly painful, and if you saw his pain—well, you can't, nor do you want to, I'm sure, as I don't want to see it, nor can Sam bear to look at himself. Nor, of course, can his grad student, who has since transferred to a smaller college back east. I've been told eventually the disease will kill him, though not for five to ten years, perhaps.

Does it matter, the reality of either of our lives? What matters is this list. Sam's disease, by the way, is the reason we have no picture of the family this year, only a group of four Christmas trees perched on a snow-covered hillside at sunrise—a photo I won a prize for at the local art center. The photo is the main thing, that and the signature. Maybe you'll notice that Sam's is a little shakier than usual.

I think Timothy, our oldest, has become a sugar addict. He spends his allowance on sweet breakfast cereals, and spends most of his time in his room eating box after box of Sugar Smacks, Honeycombs, and Count Chocula while writing plays that he rehearses and performs in private, to an audience of one. The only reason I know he's writing plays is because I've found them while cleaning and have heard him rehearsing, playing the part of director as well as star. "Now, let's try that again with a little more passion," he'll cry out as I pass by in the hall. He's very secretive about these plays, and would be upset if he knew I knew (much less told you) about their existence. But I mention his plays, not to denigrate them or express my concern, but because this is something, perhaps the one thing in my family, of which I'm truly proud, other than Corrine's courage in regard to her missing foot. I'm proud of him because of his strength, because I can see that he's taking something twisted and fashioning it into something to help him adapt and survive. Someday he'll want an audience, maybe, but for now he's content to keep the stage small and fragile and true.

So unlike me, I think. So unlike Sam and even Corrine. So unlike all of us who need this audience, this holiday affirmation that's not so much about greeting as applause, stage-setting, curtains rising and falling.

Yes, it's been an eventful year for all of us. Though we don't eat dinner together anymore, we can all help out with the mailing of these cards. It's tradition, and Sam and I insist that the kids help out. I write the letters, Corrine addresses them. Tim and I lick the stamps and Corrine and Sam seal the envelopes. Even this year, Sam won't forsake his duty of sealing the envelopes, though each movement is agony for him. Each year, the list grows. Each year, we send out the letter and the cards a little earlier. This year, perhaps I will smile at them all and stop what I'm doing. I'll probably look crazily happy and proud of them all. This one time a year, we have come together again to send out our letter to the known world, to exchange greetings, to remain on the list, to feel we know you.

Wishing you all the happiness and joy of the season.

The Delarges.
SamJean, Timothy, Corrine

The Underwater Town

What Jan remembers of the underwater town is this: she and her former husband—former *boyfriend*—Ethan, standing on the shore of the lake and casting stones where the steeple might be, guessing outcomes. Two children, not their own, had accompanied them to that shore, Leslie kneeling, Walt sorting through rocks to skim, and Jan remembers thinking how ruined and old these children were, how their parents could never do enough to make amends. She remembers her own resolve to be strong and parental, and how the mistakes of others hit her like refracted sunlight. She felt like a visionary, a rock in her hand, sure that wherever she aimed, she was bound to strike something hidden, the secret button that would make Atlantis rise again. She was twenty-one. Revelation had seemed as sure as blood.

Of course, she couldn't have been thinking all of this at the time. Feeling it, perhaps, but not thinking, so it's not a lie exactly.

If she were being honest with herself, she'd probably tell you that this weekend, except for the ruined children, was the happiest she's ever been, that things were in order, that she felt she had an advantage over the rest of creation. But she can't completely remember it this way. She knows what happened next. A year later, one month before she was married, Ethan introduced her to the woman he was sleeping with, though Jan didn't know who this woman was at the time. It took three more months for her to uncover that bald fact, and it still must stun her today. What she can't understand is how Ethan could set up their life in one way, and at the same time destroy it so carefully, like some roofer shingling half the house while leaving the other half to rot in the elements.

Jacob Berlin, Ethan's teacher, had asked the two of them to house-sit for him and his wife. She and Ethan had only been dating three months. "We have to get along," he had said with such solemnity, earnestly kissing the back of her hand, that she believed he was speaking with some kind of divine authority. He had already told her twice before that he wanted to spend the rest of his life with her—not exactly a proposal, or at least she didn't take it that way. The first time he said it was three minutes after they met. Ethan was the kind of person who charms others and himself with his own extravagance, whose enthusiasm for everything annoys some people while others feel beautiful and alive in his presence. Ethan proposed a dry run, a Whitman's Sampler of marriage, complete with a dream home and two kids—a nine-year-old boy and a thirteen-year-old girl.

Jan didn't know Jacob Berlin well. He was a delicate man with thinning blond hair, a goatee, and a brittle and elegant mustache. Jacob and Ethan went out drinking sometimes and shot pool. Ethan came back flushed and stumbling from these outings, saying what a great guy Jacob was, and how they talked about anything and everything. There wasn't the wall between them that usually existed between students and professors. Ethan came from a small town in Indiana, and Jacob came from Massachusetts. He'd lived in Bloomington for seventeen years, but told Ethan he still didn't feel like he lived in Indiana. "It's where my job is, where I have my home and family, but I don't *live* here."

When Jan thinks of the house, she thinks sunken and green. She thinks levels. Natural light all around. The house was in the middle of a forest, up a long hill. A deck surrounded the second floor, and invading tree limbs crowded around.

Jacob's son, Walt, answered the door. He was a curly-headed boy with a large nose and full lips. "I'm in the middle of something," he said in greeting, cracking the door open just enough to let them slip in. She and Ethan, holding hands, smiled at each other. Inside, Walt turned and walked away. "We're all in the middle of something." He opened a door and ran down some stairs.

The other members of the family, looking as though they'd been posed a moment before, sat or stood at their various stations around the living room. Jacob Berlin sat on a Mission-style couch, watching a fishing program on a large-screen TV.

His wife stood by a picture window that looked on the forest. She wasn't looking out the window, but rather, grimly at her daughter, Leslie, who was seated at a piano playing a frail piece of music with a kind of Rachmaninoff intensity.

No one made a move, though Jacob turned and smiled briefly. It was as though Jan and Ethan were making a delivery, and no one really wanted to sign for whatever package they were handing over. But Ethan didn't let it bother him. Still holding her hand, he led her toward Jacob.

"This is Jan," he said to the room.

Although she was completely unacquainted with this family, except for the briefest of meetings with Jacob, it somehow fell upon her to take the house-sitting tour with Tess, Jacob's wife, while Ethan and Jacob sat on the couch with a couple of beers and chatted manically.

Tess had lists everywhere, yellow Post-it notes posted on seemingly every available surface, even inside the refrigerator: "Finish the Gouda but leave the Camembert." "Leslie likes 2%, but Walt will only drink skim." "The half and half is for you."

Tess had a kind of hardened beauty that Jan didn't think of as beautiful at all, but perverse and mean. To her, beauty lay in how open and vulnerable you made yourself. Tess was a tall brunette who looked as though Coco Chanel herself had made her up. The overall effect of her was monochromatic, peach. She wore a short skirt and a jacket with pocket flaps and a braided trim. Around her neck she wore long chains of pearl and gold. Her hair was in a French twist and her earrings were teardrop pearls. She carried a shoulder bag with a chain strap, stocked no doubt with just the right eyeshadow and blush and, of course, plenty of Chanel #5. She did not look to Jan like a professor's wife. She expected someone more disheveled, bohemian-looking, the life of the mind, all that.

Jan knew things about this woman that she couldn't tell her. Jacob shared confidences with Ethan, who then shared them with Jan. Tess had had liposuction and breast implants. She colored her hair. Her belly button was an "outty." Ethan swore he had never divulged anything about his private life with Jan, except for small things like the sexual positions they favored. He was being serious, but those kinds of things rolled off his tongue so unabashedly that they seemed funny and almost inconsequential.

The last stop was the garden, which smelled of mint, and was a tangle of herbs and ground cover and daisies. There were no Post-it notes here, though the yellow centers of the daisies almost looked like them. Tess didn't say anything, but smiled for the first time, took a deep breath, and seemed to be waiting for Jan to compliment the weeds.

"The kids will show you what to do in here," she said. "This is their territory, at least the weeding."

"It's so peaceful here," Jan said. She felt like she had to say something.

"I want that hat," Tess said, pointing to the Panama Jan wore. "You'll give it to me, right?"

Jan laughed because she almost seemed serious. She touched the brim. "Ethan and I got it at a street fair."

"Sentimental value?" she said, and from her tone Jan guessed that was not a stock she traded in. "Listen, I'll bring you back something fantastic from the Cape if you promise to give me the hat."

"If you really like it, you can have it now," Jan said, taking it off.

Tess arched her eyebrows. "You give things away too easily. I'll only take it if I come back from the Cape with something that you'd like more. Deal?"

Jan didn't want to give away her hat, and she couldn't see why Tess wanted it. This wasn't her look at all. She wouldn't look good in a Panama, and this wasn't the finest Panama in the world, either. This was a street fair Panama, a little whim on a still, hot day in August in Chicago, an endearment Ethan had given her the first month they knew each other. But Tess seemed desperate to have it, and she couldn't refuse. Jan laughed nervously and said, "It better be good."

When they returned to the living room, Leslie was still seated at the piano bench, though she wasn't playing anymore. Her brother had a chess set on the bench. He knelt on the floor, his chin in his hand while she fiddled with a little hourglass, turning it upside down every few seconds. Ethan and Jacob Berlin struggled up the hallway, each weighted down with a couple of suitcases and garment bags slung across their shoulders. They were laughing and jostling each other, trying to push past one another like stock car drivers. Jacob stopped when he saw Tess.

"What have you been doing?" she said. "The plane leaves in an hour and a half. We've still got to drive to Indy."

"The luggage," he said. "It's here. We were just taking care of it."

She shook her head. "You're so stupid."

"You play so expressively, Leslie," Jan told the girl. "What was that you were playing?"

The girl stopped fiddling with the hourglass but didn't say anything.

"That was Enrique Granados, wasn't it, Leslie?" Tess turned to Jan. "A late-nineteenth-century Spanish composer. Leslie's a Sagittarius," she added as though that explained the selection of Granados.

"Are you going to play the piano when you get older?" Jan asked.

"No," she said, looking down at her lap.

Jan flushed and said, "I meant, is it something you'd like to make a career out of."

"No," she said.

"Leslie's a brooder," her mother said.

Tess went over to kiss Walt, who sat completely still. "Don't put on a show, Mother," he said. "Call us, Daddy," he shouted. "Tonight. Call us from the airplane. You know, you can make calls from the air now."

Tess took one of the bags from Jacob and walked out the door. As soon as she was gone, the kids ran to their father and hugged him.

"Walt collects chess sets," Jacob said. "Make sure he gives you a tour. He also makes beer and wine. I encourage them to be unusual. They're both prodigies."

"So am I," Ethan said.

"You have a prodigious appetite," Jan said.

Jacob looked down at his kids, who flanked him and had their faces buried in him. The kids were both snuffling.

"I'll teach them five-card stud or strip poker if they're good," Ethan said.

"Really?" said Walt.

"They'll beat the pants off you," Jacob said. "My kids have the best poker faces in creation. Even as babies they never let us know what they were thinking."

Walt spent most of the first evening in the basement, bottling beer. Leslie, too, left them alone. She sat in the living room on the couch most of the evening, a set of earphones in. In Ethan and Jan's pretend world, the children were theirs. Jan and Ethan giggled around the house, arm-in-arm, shouting what they imagined were parental commands. First, they went to the basement and opened the door, which had a Post-it note on it. The note read in a tiny, tight script, "Walt spends all his time down here. Encourage him to come up for a breather." Jan tickled Ethan's ribs and said, "No, don't say anything."

"Okay," he said, squirming.

"I dare you," she said.

"What should I say?"

"Aunt Lois. Tell him something about his Aunt Lois."

"What if he doesn't have one."

"He's got to. I have an Aunt Lois and he's our child, so he has an Aunt Lois, too, though she's his great-aunt, I guess."

Ethan swung the door wide and leaned down the stairs. "Walt, oh Walt."

It took him about five seconds to answer. Then there was an annoyed, "What?"

"Have you written to your Aunt Lois?"

"What?" he said.

Jan covered Ethan's mouth. "I can't believe you," she said.

But Ethan was into it. He pulled Jan's hand away. "You know you're supposed to write to Aunt Lois, Walt. Have you sent her that thank you for the new . . ." Ethan turned to Jan. "The new what? Help me."

"Train set?" she said.

"No, Aunt Lois wouldn't send a train set."

"She's my aunt," Jan said.

"The new . . . microbrewery gift set, that's it."

"Aunt Lois would not send a microbrewery gift set."

"Then what?"

"A check for ten dollars," she said. For Jan, it had always been five.

Ethan gave her the thumbs-up sign and leaned again into the basement. "Have you written to thank Aunt Lois for the ten-dollar check she sent you for your birthday?"

This time, there was hardly a pause. "I did it yesterday."

Ethan slammed the door and looked at Jan. They both laughed in astonishment. "That's scary," he said. "Let's try it on Leslie."

They walked into the living room and stared at her. Her feet were on the couch and she was wearing a pair of earphones and thrumming her fingers on her leg. She didn't see them at all, or hear them, which made it easy for the attitudes they assumed.

Ethan had his arms crossed and Jan followed suit. Ethan started to say something, but she interrupted. "The girl is mine. This is a mother-daughter thing."

Ethan put his hands up and said, "Didn't mean to intrude," and started to walk away.

"No, stay," she said. "It's all right."

But he kept on walking and then she heard his footsteps on the stairs. She didn't know what to do. She felt a little ridiculous, but she also wanted to be true to the game. It seemed important that she take her role seriously. In a stage whisper, she said, "Leslie, I'm gravely disappointed. I thought I'd taught you to have more self-respect. . . ." Leslie sat up suddenly and whisked her headphones off her ears. She'd heard. Jan fled and ran up the stairs trying to contain her laughter and embarrassment. What a loon. Blame it on Ethan. He opened the door to their bedroom and she hardly needed to explain what had happened. He was laughing, too, and he opened his arms to her. "Raising a child these days is murder," she told him.

The phone rang then, and she was closest, so she answered. "Berlin household."

"It's Jacob. I'm in the air."

At first, she didn't understand what was going on. "Excuse me?"

"I'm in the air. For Christ sake, I'm in the air. Are my kids there? This is costing a fortune."

She ran to the head of the stairs. "Leslie, Walt. Your father's calling from the airplane. He's in the air."

And like a series of sentries yelling from post to post, they sounded the alarm, Walt shouting, "Leslie, it's Daddy, he's calling from the air." Leslie shouted back, "The air! The air!" like it was a battle cry, "To arms, to arms!"

At breakfast, Ethan made waffles. He and Jan were both in their bathrobes, though the children were already fully dressed.

"Did the storm wake you up last night?" Leslie asked.

Ethan and Jan looked at each other.

"It rained all night," Walt said.

Jan and Ethan hadn't even noticed, but the children had both been awakened by the thunder and crawled into bed with them. Jan half-remembered this. She thought she'd seen and felt Leslie climb into bed, but when she went back to sleep, it became part of her dream. In the morning the girl wasn't there.

"I hope the weather's good for your parents," Jan said.

"The Cape would be a nice place for a second honeymoon, or even a first," Ethan said. He held a fresh waffle by its corner and he ran it over to Jan.

"I've never been to the Cape," she said.

"We have," said Leslie.

"It's not a second honeymoon anyway," said Walt. "They're getting a divorce. They're just going to work out the details."

Leslie wriggled in her seat and she and her brother exchanged looks.

"It's all right," said Walt. "They fight about everything. They fought about a hammer."

Leslie started giggling.

"Leslie, stop it," said Walt. "It's not that funny." Then he turned back to Jan. "I hope they don't change their minds. I hope they're not to going to try to give us another little brother or sister. I'd hate to see them fall into that trap."

"There wasn't really a storm last night," Leslie said.

"Leslie," her brother scolded.

"We heard you making love," she said.

"Leslie, there are some things that are private," Jan said.

"Not anymore," Walt said. "Daddy says nothing is private anymore in America."

Ethan looked seriously at the children. "That sounds like your dad, but some things *are* private, solemn, sacred even."

Leslie started giggling again until milk came out of her nose. After she'd calmed down she said, "I don't think you'll last the weekend with us, but Walt does."

"Don't tell them everything," Walt said, and he stood up to leave the table. Leslie followed his lead.

"You forgot something," Ethan said, pointing to their dishes.

"What?" said Walt.

"We're going to get along just fine," Ethan said, "but only as long as you pay attention to what we say. Your mother said you had to listen to us." Jan liked this side of Ethan. Usually, he didn't believe in setting limits, for himself or anyone else.

"Her word doesn't carry a lot of weight around here," Walt said.

Ethan brought Jan's hand to his lips and started kissing her arm. Jan thought she knew where he was going with this. She could read his mind, could almost hear his clear voice say, "Play along. Let's teach these kids a lesson."

"Oh Ethan," she said, and started panting. They kissed in the exaggerated ways of old movies, what they called "a movie kiss," their mouths smashing together, then turning sideways cheek to cheek so that the camera could see the intensity of their passion.

Ethan placed a hand under her terry cloth robe and lifted her while still trying to kiss—a little awkward, but they managed—onto the kitchen table. He cleared away some of the dishes with his other hand, and she tried to kick things away with her leg. She felt something under her back. It gave way like some tiny mattress and spread out—a stick of butter. She couldn't see the reaction of the kids. She was trying too hard to make sure that most of her stayed inside the robe. Her bare leg dangled over the side of the table.

The kids didn't make a sound. "Ethan," she said.

"Well, you get the idea," said Ethan, sitting up and adjusting his robe.

Walt looked at them blankly, like he'd simply been watching TV. "That was very educational," he said. "Can we go now?"

Leslie had a completely different look on her face: a little confused, but she was smiling, and her hands were up to her face in a prayer position. She was hunched slightly forward as though she wanted a better look. The intensity of her expression embarrassed Jan.

Jan sat up and her foot brushed something. She felt it tip off the table. There was a crash.

"My mom just bought that milk pitcher at Ethan Allen," said Walt.

"I'm going to do some weeding," Leslie said.

"They're not human," Ethan said after the kids had left. "I was sure they'd freak out."

Jan picked up a shard of the pitcher they'd broken, and noticed a Post-it note on it. The Post-it note didn't read, "This is a shard," as she expected. It read, "Not for everyday use."

"Our children won't be like that," said Ethan as he stacked plates and cups by the sink. "They'll freak out on command, won't they?"

"If we have children," Jan said.

"Not have children?" he said. He looked out the window. "I always thought I'd have children, three or four even."

"Maybe you will," she said.

Jan found her Panama hat and put it on. It seemed like a good garden hat. Maybe that's why Tess wanted it. When she found Leslie, the girl was kneeling in the middle of a tangle of weeds and flowers, digging with a little trowel. She stood up when she saw Jan and gave her a pair of her mother's gloves and another trowel. Then she went back to her work while Jan just stood there waiting, not knowing where to begin. "Maybe you can show me a few tricks."

"I don't have any tricks," Leslie said. "It's been pretty badly neglected. None of us really have had the time, and all Walt cares about is his stupid beer-making these days. I don't even know why he makes it. He hates the taste of it. My mother doesn't drink it, and Dad only drinks low-calorie beer."

"Maybe he likes the process," Jan said, not really knowing what she was saying.

But that seemed like the right thing. Leslie turned around, smiled, and brushed her hair from her eyes. It was the first really genuine smile Jan had seen from either of the children, a smile that didn't have any irony attached. She wanted to tell Leslie what a lovely smile she had, but she didn't want to push it.

"Sure," Leslie said. "That's what I like about this. I never seem to get anywhere, but I don't care. I just like doing it."

Jan knelt down in the middle of the weed patch beside the child. She picked off a stray Post-it note from her pants. It read, "Sump pump in basement."

"That's ground cover," Leslie said as soon as Jan started digging. "Ground cover is our friend." She laughed. She took Jan's hand and guided her to a little clump of grass. With her hand around Jan's she guided the trowel deep around the plant. "There," she said. "That's it. You want to make sure you don't leave any root behind. They're tenacious little boogers. That's what my mom calls them." She laughed again, pleasantly. Jan smiled but was afraid to laugh, afraid she might startle her. She just let Leslie guide her hand until she understood what to do on her own.

That night in bed, Ethan was shy. He didn't want to make love again while they were there.

"Why not?" Jan asked.

"I don't want to set a bad example," he said.

"Bad example?" Jan said.

She heard something, like a muffled explosion. She went out into the hall and in the dimness she made out a shape.

"Walt?"

He stood by the banister, looking down. "My beer," he said. "A bad batch. Autolysis."

"What's that?"

"The yeast runs out of sugar and it starts cannibalizing itself."

"Is there anything I can do?" she asked, as though she could prevent yeast from cannibalizing itself.

"No," he said. "But thank you for your concern. You can return to your room now. I'm just going to wait up a little longer. There's really nothing that can be done."

She went over to him and touched his hair. He stood there vigilant, waiting for the next explosion, but he didn't seem to mind her touching him. He looked up at her and she said, "Go to sleep soon." Then she returned to the room where Ethan was waiting for her and told him all about autolysis and Walt's parental concern for his cannibalistic yeast.

"They're strange kids," she whispered, "but there's something sweet about them, too."

Ethan laughed and said, "I told you so," though he had, in fact, told her nothing.

She dreamed of rain, but in the morning, there was no sign of it. She questioned Ethan, and he told her that he, too, had thought it rained. But the kids told them no, that all they'd probably heard was the sound of the wind in the trees surrounding the house. Jan also thought that Leslie had climbed into bed with her again, but this time she didn't ask. There wasn't any point in asking. Everything was off-balance in that house. Bottles exploded. It rained or it didn't rain. Who could tell for sure? The children simply needed . . . what? Stability, even if it came from strangers, even if there was no future in it. A sort of free-floating guilt permeated the house, and they all needed to get away.

So they drove, took a family outing to a lake Jacob had told Ethan about, a secret place he'd never brought anyone to. It was a reservoir that had once been a town, but twenty-five years ago, it had been covered with water and all the inhabitants had been moved, had been scattered. From the shore of the lake, they couldn't see anything. It looked like just another lake, but the mystery captivated them. The lake was about seven miles long, and they had no idea where the flooded town was, if it was anywhere near the shore where they stood.

They ate their lunch by the shore. Walt brought some of his beer, a good batch, a porter that he'd made. Jan and Ethan each had a couple. Even though she didn't normally like dark beer, this had a rich molasses taste and a subtle sweetness. They told Walt how much they liked it but he didn't seem to believe them.

"You really like it?" he said.

"Yes, Walt," Jan said. "I've already told you. It's great."

"How would you describe it? Would you describe it as woody?"

"I would describe it as oaky," said Ethan.

"Maybe walnutty," Jan said.

"Teak-like," said Ethan.

The beach was pebbly, except for one man-sized limestone rock that jutted into the water. After lunch, Ethan climbed on top of it and scanned the surface. "Look," Ethan said. "Come here. I see the town under the water."

Walt scrambled up the rock and looked where Ethan pointed. "Liar," he said and laughed. "There's nothing there."

"Sure there is," Ethan said. "I can see the church."

Leslie climbed up with a wary look and Jan followed. Jan knew Ethan. She didn't believe him for a moment. "Where?" Leslie asked.

"Actually, I can see the front door from up here," Ethan said. "There's a sign that says, 'Mothers' Morning Out—Wednesday, August 21.' Hey, that's tomorrow."

"There's the bank," Jan said.

"Where?"

"Over there by that water lily."

"And there's the courthouse right across from the bank."

They pretended they could see the entire layout. Ethan had always had that confident ability to project himself into a different world, the conviction that the truth of predictions didn't matter, that there was beauty enough in the attempt. And that's in part what Jan loved about him. She'd grown up in a family of outcomes, not predictions.

"I don't believe this," Walt said. He scanned the water and said, "I don't see a thing. You're just teasing."

"Keep looking," Ethan said. "You'll see something eventually."

"You see anything, Leslie?" Walt asked.

"A man in a canoe," she said.

She pointed, right into the sun, but after a while, Jan's eyes adjusted, and she saw a canoe coming around a wooded bend, heading toward an inlet not more than a hundred yards away. The man wore a straw hat, the kind with crazy frills going every which way. The canoe was silver and glinted in the sun. The man, overweight and in his sixties, seemed determined to get somewhere. The canoe turned and he went out of the sun for a moment. Jan imagined fishing gear and fish on a string in the bow.

"Where do you think he's going?" Leslie asked.

"Let's call out to him," said Walt. "Let's ask."

Jan put her hands up to her mouth to hail the man. "Wait," Ethan said, touching her arm. "Maybe we shouldn't bother him."

"I want to see what kind of fish those are," Jan said.

"What fish?"

"In the bow of the canoe."

"Those are flowers," Ethan said.

She looked at him. "What would he be doing with flowers? Those are fish. Clearly, he caught some fish and now he's going to another fishing hole."

"They're flowers," Ethan said. "Definitely flowers. I've got it all figured out. His wife is buried here in a little cemetery. They used to live in the underwater town before it was flooded, and the cemetery is the only thing that remains above water. The only way he can reach it is by canoe."

"That's very dear," Jan said. "But he's bringing her fish."

The canoeist disappeared into the dark inlet, moving silently out of the sunlight and out of earshot. But she saw him in profile, his head bent in reverie or sorrow, or perhaps he was just studying a lure on the floor of the canoe that they couldn't see.

"What did you see?" Ethan asked Walt.

"It's too far away," he said. "How can you see anything?"

"What did you see, Leslie?" Jan asked.

"Flowers," she said and leapt off the rock.

Jan felt disappointed she couldn't imagine the flowers. She'd rather have seen flowers in the canoe. She preferred Ethan's version. It was a good story, and it made her happy that Ethan had thought of it, that he could imagine such devotion. She wanted to imagine him in that canoe even though it meant her own death. But maybe through grand gestures he could retrieve her or die trying. She'd be waiting for him in that underwater town, like Eurydice waiting for Orpheus to lead her back to the world.

Jan climbed off the rock and stood by the water's edge, away from the rest of them. She picked up a smooth stone and rubbed it in her hands.

She felt his hands on her shoulders. "What are you thinking of?" he asked.

She stepped aside. With a sidelong whipping motion, she tossed the rock in the water. It skimmed the surface, dodging like a water bug.

"Wow," Ethan said. "Where'd you learn that? You must have skipped it at least five times."

"Don't exaggerate," she said. "It was four."

"Hey, you want to skip stones?" Ethan called to the kids. Walt was washing his bottles in the lake and Leslie was sitting on the rock still, picking apart the veins of a fallen leaf. Each child seemed in a bit of a trance, as though skipping stones were some onerous duty they had to perform simply because they were children and it was expected of them. As Jan watched them amble over, she knew she would never make such mistakes with her children. She would not introduce them to guests as prodigies. Of course, she and Ethan would fight sometimes, but she wouldn't let the children be exposed to their recriminations. No one would be the villain. No one would have to take sides. She could sense in their faces, like age lines, every single mistake their parents had made over the years. To her, they didn't look or act like children. They were bent and wizened, shouldering all the pain their parents had foisted on them.

Jan did most of the skimming. Ethan couldn't get the hang of it, and so he started bombarding the underwater town with rocks. Jan imagined the underwater people looking up curiously at this mini-Pompeii, Ethan's rocks showering down on them, disturbing their world, kicking up silt and muddying the water. This irritated her, but she said nothing. She simply kept her rocks above the fray.

Walt, the little perfectionist, spent most of his time searching the shore for just the right rocks to skim, and so avoided the possibility of actually having to throw a rock and watch it sink.

Leslie, the silent watcher, knelt down beside Jan with her leaf. When she was through dissecting it, she set it aside and leaned back. "Do you think there's something down there?" she asked.

Jan turned just as Ethan hurled his rock across the water.

"What?" Jan asked Leslie.

"The town. Do you think it's really down there?"

"Jan! Did you catch that?" Ethan was whooping and hollering. "That must have skipped seven times."

"No honey, I'm sorry," she said. "I didn't see."

"You didn't see? Seven times," he said. He picked up another rock and plunked it into the water by his feet. "Your turn," he said.

"Sure it's down there," Jan told Leslie, who was still looking up expectantly, like Jan had all the answers. And she felt she did.

"It wasn't *really* seven," Ethan told her, shuffling his feet a bit. "But it took four *really* good hops. It felt like seven."

"Step aside," Jan said. "Give the master room. Five hops," she announced. She planned to put everything into her throw. If her stone skipped five times then she and Ethan would be happily married and their children would be well-adjusted.

Walt, down the beach, raised his hand triumphantly. "I found one. I found a great one." He dashed toward them, stopped, examined his rock again, and said more softly, "No, this one's not right either."

And then she threw.

When they returned, they saw the car in the driveway. The four of them were silent from their first glimpse of the car to the moment they set eyes on Jacob and Tess. They expected the couple to be angry, upset with one another, but they were sitting on the couch arm-in-arm when the four others entered. Tess had on Jan's Panama hat and Jacob was holding one of Walt's chess pieces, a rook, rolling it around in his fingers.

"Why did you come home so early?" Leslie asked. The four of them stood gaping at Tess and Jacob, sitting there like some young couple in love. They seemed like oddities, like a parody of a couple in love, aliens who haven't quite mastered human form yet. Jan didn't know what this meant. She thought they'd gone away to talk about the terms of their divorce. Their renewed affection felt unnatural, and it threw off Jan's perception of the children.

"We were anxious to get home . . . to you," Jacob said, standing up and walking over to them with the castle in his hand, his arms open for a hug.

Leslie turned from him and ran instead to Tess, still sitting on the couch. She dove into her mother's arms like a three-year-old. Tess looked shocked, then laughed. She lightly touched her daughter's back and looked at them like some amazed fisher who's just had a fish leap into his boat.

"What a welcome," she said, not to Leslie, but to Jan and Ethan.

Jacob tried to give Walt a hug, but was rebuffed, not as strongly as Leslie, but Walt squirmed away, his eyes on his sister. The way Leslie and Walt interacted was so strange. They observed each other so carefully, studied each other, as though they were colleagues with great mutual respect for one another's work. Walt walked over to where Tess was sitting, with Leslie still buried in her lap, knelt down, and placed his head against his mother's arm. Then he closed his eyes. Tentatively, she touched his cheek. She started to stroke his hair. "Mother," he said softly. "Don't pet me. I'm not a dog."

Tess took her hand away like she'd burned it, and laughed again, high-pitched and nervous. "Of course you're not," she said. She looked at Ethan and Jan and then at Jacob, befuddlement and apology in her eyes.

Jacob acted as though he hadn't suddenly been rejected by his children, like he'd been meaning to simply come over to where Jan and Ethan stood.

"How was the weekend? Any problems?" Jacob said.

"We broke one of your milk pitchers," Ethan said, "while we were up on the kitchen table. Besides that, just a little autolysis. Other than that, everything was great."

Jacob nodded like Ethan made perfect sense. He didn't even want to know what they were doing on the table. He didn't even care what autolysis had to do with anything. No one knew Ethan as well as Jan did at that moment. Or so she thought. He was letting Jan know in his own way that none of this mattered, that it wasn't their concern, that they had their own mysteries between them. The words they used had previously been defined by the other.

Jan wanted to leave the house as soon as possible, and so she went upstairs to pack. Ethan offered to help but she told him to stay, to enjoy himself, it wouldn't take her long. Actually, she didn't want anyone's company. She didn't know what she wanted. She wanted another day, just her and Ethan and the kids. Tess and Jacob's early arrival had spoiled things. Just that afternoon she'd been so sure of everything. The kids had detested their mother before she left, and now they clung to her? Tess and Jacob had gone away to talk about the terms of their divorce, and now they were in love again? She felt tricked, betrayed, foolish. They hadn't gone away to talk about their divorce. They'd just gone away for the weekend together—a second honeymoon like she had first assumed.

When she returned downstairs, dragging her suitcase behind her, the confusion showed on her face. No one said a word to her. Tess and Ethan sat on the couch, laughing, and Walt was in Tess' lap.

"I should get my hat," Jan said to Tess.

Tess looked alarmed, but she smiled. "Oh, I thought we had a bargain."

Jan wiggled her head a bit.

"Actually, the hat means something to me," she said, "and I'd like to keep it. It was the first thing Ethan ever gave me."

"Of course," Tess said gently. "You're right to keep it." She took it off and Walt scooted off her lap. He was looking at Jan curiously with almost the same studiousness as he regarded his sister.

"I brought you something back from the Cape," Tess told Jan.

"That's all right."

"No, I want you to have it. Maybe it will have some sentimental value to you someday." She went to her purse, dug around, and pulled out a green candle the shape and size of a frog. She laughed and handed Jan the candle and the hat. Jan didn't say anything at first. She didn't know what to say. She wasn't sure that anything, or very little, meant much to this woman or the rest of her mysterious family.

"Kinky," Ethan said and laughed.

"It was funny," Tess said. "You seem to appreciate irony."

Jan managed to tell her how thoughtful it was of her to buy her this frog candle.

It was time to leave. Jan said good-bye to Walt. They shook hands in the polite and formal way he had about him.

"Have you seen Leslie?" Jan asked.

"Maybe she's in the basement," Tess said, pointing. "I saw Jacob go down there."

The basement door was open. Jan could hear an electric humming coming from it, and a shimmering light was cast through the open door. That was the only part of the house she hadn't seen, but it was too late now. She stood at the top of the stairs and looked down the steep staircase, but didn't have a view except for a few yards of the concrete floor, and what looked like a foot of water covering it. Above the noise of the humming, she heard what sounded like a waterfall. A beer bottle, like a channel marker, bobbed at the bottom. She called Leslie from the top of the stairs. She heard splashing and Jacob appeared.

"Is the basement flooded?" she asked.

"The basement's flooded?" Tess said from the couch.

Walt let out an anguished moan and said, "It was dry yesterday." He came over to where Jan stood and looked down into the basement. "My beer must be ruined," he said.

"Your beer's ruined," said Jacob.

"Not necessarily," said Tess, touching his hair, then pulling back and putting a hand on his arm.

"No, it's all ruined," Jacob said. "I knew something would happen if we left. And now Walt's beer is ruined." He spoke like a man in deepest despair, as though Walt's beer meant the world to him. "Didn't anyone mention the sump pump?" he asked Jan and went away.

"You have to admit, darling," Tess said to Walt, "that no one drinks your beer anyway, so even if it's ruined technically, it's still a perfect batch as long as no one opens it. Right? It's like one of those tree-falls-in-the-forest things."

"Why won't you drink my beer?" he asked, holding his mother's hand as the two of them went down the stairs.

"You have to understand, sweetheart. I just don't like beer."

"Maybe wine?" he asked.

"Maybe," and they splashed out of sight.

"Sump pump," Jan said. The phrase was familiar. She'd seen it written down somewhere.

"Can we help?" Ethan yelled.

No one answered him.

"What's going on?" Jan jumped at the sound of Leslie's voice.

"I was looking for you, Leslie!" Jan said. Leslie stopped at the sound of her name and looked as though Jan had said something foreign.

"I guess you found me," she said.

"I wanted to say good-bye," Jan said.

She gave Jan a hug, but it felt stiff, obligatory. Jan wanted to say, I thought you liked me. Wasn't I good to you? She held onto the girl a moment too long. Ethan interrupted. "The basement's flooded," he told her.

"Cool," Leslie said, letting go, and took off her shoes and socks and ran downstairs. She turned around at the bottom and waved.

"Miss me," she said.

They could have gone down and joined them, helped them clean up. They heard them splashing and laughing like a family at the seashore, riding waves, having water fights.

Jacob rose up the steps and closed the door quietly behind him. "Oh," he said when he saw Jan and Ethan. "Thanks a lot," and he shook Ethan's hand and then Jan's. She could tell what Ethan was thinking, that house-sitting hadn't reinforced his position in Jacob's inner circle, and that's all he'd really wanted, to be an intimate part of his professor's world. The weekend had had the opposite effect, had banished him. "Mind if I send you the check?" Jacob asked as he kept climbing, rising through the levels of the house, but the question wasn't a question at all. It was a buried statement. He meant, "You know your way out." Ethan looked devastated.

Looking upstairs is her last reliable memory of that weekend, Jacob walking to his study as though invisible. He held something in his hands. She couldn't see what. She thought of the man in the canoe gliding toward a destination the rest of them could only guess at.

She couldn't have imagined that only eighteen months later she'd be married and divorced. Most people don't know she was married for six months. She feels no need to tell them. She's tried to block it out. If she really wanted to understand Ethan's reasons, she would have to go so far into his mind that she would never see the light of day again. But she doesn't. Really, it ended almost as soon as she and Ethan returned from their honeymoon. They weren't married long. The wink of an eye. She doesn't have anything good to say about him now. She's lost all her respect for him. He can't have much self-respect either.

Two weeks later, Tess and Jacob announced they were getting a divorce. The children had been telling the truth. Their parents hadn't gone away for a second honeymoon, but to discuss their separation. And now that it was decided, they walked around arm-in-arm in public, or holding hands, like first lovers in tight martial formation, desperate for the press of flesh, a violence in their eyes. For them there was an infatuation period before the divorce. Jan couldn't imagine such a strain of happiness. Maybe they had fought and called each other horrible names when they first met. Maybe for them, everything was backward, flipped upside down. Their children, anyway, seemed to be growing backward, from stunted ancients to vulnerable infants.

Today, let's imagine Jan writing a letter to Leslie, a card from her and Ethan. She tells her about her child, about the garden she's started, the weeding tips she learned from Leslie. But of course, Jan wouldn't lie, wouldn't really write something like that—even though somewhere inside her, maybe it's true.

Let's wonder about her. She's thirty-one now. The frog candle, which she ended up with, is ten. The Panama hat. Who knows what happened to it? It was lost. What's important keeps changing. Let's say that the frog candle is still intact, that she has been unable to light that candle until now. Let's do it for her, help her light it and let go of that afternoon before things went wrong, on the cusp of rightness.

The underwater town is rising. The man in the canoe brushes right past it, unaware. Let's think of other things. Let's think only of surfaces, the skin of the water and the lip of the rock meeting, that indelible moment when the seemingly impossible happens and something that should sink leaps back for a moment into the air.

Redemption

The first time they heard the preacher, Dan and Molly were about to make love. Molly had her arms around Dan's neck. They were on the four-poster flea market bed, both of them paint-spackled and exhausted from a day of fixing up the new bungalow. Sex had been about the farthest thing from either of their minds. They'd been discussing color schemes for the bedroom, Dan quite seriously, Molly only half-heartedly. "You choose," she'd said with impatience and indifference edging her voice. "Whatever it is, it'll be fine." Dan felt his own irritation and joylessness rise inside him, and almost answered her sharply. Instead, he beat his anger back. Molly, defiant, ready to fight, but willing to avoid one, said, partly as a diversionary tactic, partly as an irritation test, "You know, you've got paint all over your new glasses." The two of them stood side by side, waiting, poised between rejection and need, and then toppled together into bed. This promised to be the best kind of lovemaking: wholly unplanned, intuitive, wild, and slightly comical.

In the quiet moment before starting to shed their work clothes, in that moment when both wanted to savor the gentle victory of need over rejection, they heard a voice, insistent as the creak of the bed.

"*Abomination!*" The voice seemed fierce as a battle cry, and curdled the air around them.

Dan scrambled up, kneeing Molly in the stomach. Molly sat up and crossed an arm over her breasts though she was fully clothed.

Dan put a hand through his hair and stared at the door as though waiting for someone to burst into the room.

"Was that you?" Molly said.

Dan shook his head and slowly got up. He picked up an old medicine bottle off the dresser. The bottle was another flea market purchase. Molly had bought it for him. Made of heavy glass, the bottle had stamped on it, "The Great Doctor Kilmer's Swamp Root Kidney Liver Bladder Cure." For him, it was kind of a strange reminder of the days when he used to drink, before he met Molly. These old medicines had contained mostly alcohol. Stamped "Cure," people had actually trusted them. Dan was skeptical of cures. He felt the opposite of the belief that "whatever doesn't kill you makes you stronger." He believed that whatever you *need* to make you stronger or better or healthier or happier will kill you. He held the bottle by the neck and stalked through the rooms of the house, but found no intruder. When he returned, he shrugged his shoulders and said, "Must be a ghost."

Molly smiled, buoyed by his bravado. "I hear they can't harm you unless you're afraid of them. Hey, Mr. Ghost, watch this." She started to unbutton her work shirt.

Neither Dan nor Molly doubted what they'd heard, and neither thought the other had yelled "Abomination," but their fatigue and irritation gave them a kind of devil-may-care attitude. Anyway, this was their house. They'd just moved in. They'd barely been able to scrape together the down payment. If not for some help from Dan's mother, they'd still be renting.

So they went ahead. They made love, though now it seemed more planned, more purposeful, and the whole time Molly and Dan kept their eyes closed, not wanting to look past each other's body.

Both Dan and Molly were skeptical people, people of common sense, not among the 80 percent or so of the American public who believe in UFOs. But they were among the 90 percent who read their daily horoscopes, though both would have denied actually believing in such things. Still, if Molly's horoscope read, "You will receive an unexpected call," she immediately thought of all the people who might call her unexpectedly.

They were startled by the thought of a ghost, but not frightened. Dan grew up Baptist and Molly Presbyterian. Now they attended Unitarian services but considered themselves agnostic. Molly, who was ten years older than he was, had straightened him out a long time ago when he was still drinking. Possessed by drink. Jobless, virtually homeless, suicidal. He owed her his life. He had seen walking ghosts before. He had been one. Molly had brought him back to life.

A week later, Molly was lying in bed, waiting for Dan to come in from the living room where he was watching TV. She was reading a book, but she kept glancing at the walls. Dan had chosen peach. Peach just didn't work in here. It wasn't a bright peach, but a drab peach, kind of a rotten peach, and she just couldn't stand looking at the color anymore. But Dan wasn't the kind of person who liked to be corrected. He'd say they couldn't afford to paint the room with a different color now, and anyway, she'd had her chance to have some input. "But the ghost distracted me," she said as an excuse to herself, imagining a heated argument with Dan. "Really," she imagined him saying with that sarcastic edge she just hated. "Blaming it on a ghost. You had your chance."

Molly put her book down and clicked off the light on the bedside table, feeling slightly irritated with Dan, though their argument had only been imagined this time. She felt herself drifting off and someone sat down on the edge of her bed.

"Dan?"

"I . . . I am he that comforts you," said a voice loudly and rhythmically. "Who are you that you are afraid of man who dies?"

Molly brought her legs up and pulled the bedcovers.

"Dan!" she yelled. A ball of light, red and green and tacky-looking, like a lava lamp, floated above her bed.

"And they shall go forth and look on the dead bodies of the men that have rebelled against me; for their worm shall not die, their fire shall not be quenched, and they shall be an abhorrence to all flesh."

Dan stood now in the doorway. He had been asleep in front of the TV when, hearing Molly's yell, he bolted up, running down the hallway half asleep, to see this apparition in front of their bed.

"Who are you?" Molly asked.

"There are two religions in the world and only two," the apparition announced. "One is the religion of busyness and worldliness, the religion of self-actualization and idolatry, and then there is the religion of Jesus Christ. Those are the only two."

An old smell hung in the air. Dan couldn't quite place it, something from long ago, from his childhood in Asheville, North Carolina.

"Sweet potato pie!" he yelled. His voice seemed to break the spell and the apparition shut off. Like a TV picture, it collapsed on itself into a tiny white dot, which lingered a moment and then blinked out. But the smell stayed, like room freshener.

Dan wasn't sure what to do. He stood in the darkness, his eyes adjusting. "Are you all right?" he asked Molly.

She wanted him to touch her, but there seemed a gulf between them, and she couldn't find her voice to talk. If she talked, whatever need in her she felt would be quashed. But she also didn't want to be touched, felt watched, disapproved of, and knew that whatever Dan did right now would be wrong.

"I think I'll just try to go to sleep," she said. "I don't think he'll be back."

Dan crossed the room and sat on the edge of the bed. He reached out lightly, as if his hand might go through her, and stroked her arm distractedly.

"Don't touch me now," she said. She felt old, unbeautiful, decaying. She saw herself in the grave, her arms folded primly across her chest.

And Dan felt the decay in the room, too, but was able to transform it, remembered a time early in their life together when they went apple-picking, how he cried in her arms in the deep orchard, the wet smell of decaying leaves and rotten apples surrounding them. He remembered crying because he had been so wrong, hadn't cared, hadn't seen life's possibilities until a few days earlier when Molly had taken him for coffee and recognized that he wasn't past redemption. She had stayed up all night with him, talking, casting away his self-doubts one by one like rags until he was naked and could see all he'd missed, how blind he'd been in his alcoholic state. And he saw that he wasn't going to die, that it mattered, that she cared, and it all came together in that orchard as he kissed her for the first time through his tears.

Now, remembering, he bent down over her and fighting through her own rejection and self-loathing, came to kiss her with tenderness and thanksgiving—and the memory passed through his lips onto hers, became a taste, a berry that burst over and through her. And the two of them were so glad they had found one another, and this house was so perfect for them except for one thing, which they forced from their minds while they made love.

"I hate peach," she admitted to him the next day. He was building a fire in the wood stove. She was cutting up construction paper Halloween decorations for the neighborhood kids. She loved children but could never have any and blamed herself, though there was nothing she could have done except go back into time to the hospital when she was seventeen and had lost her first and only child. If she could have gone back into time, she would have begged God not to do that to her because it had scarred her for life, and now she couldn't have any children. And the experience had made her hate God for so many years and hate herself and then settle down into not caring until this moment when the pang returned because Dan would have made such a good father. He was patient and good and trusting. But this was all nonverbal and took place in a flash in her mind and was transformed into the words, "I hate peach."

"What?" Dan said. He was crumpling up a newspaper, stuffing it into the deepest recess of the wood stove.

"I want to change the color of the bedroom," she said, thinking of the baby she'd never even seen.

Dan didn't say anything. He shrugged his shoulders imperceptibly and took his arm out of the stove.

"I think it's a stupid color," Molly said. "I'll go crazy if I have to sleep in a peach bedroom. It makes me feel like a pit."

Dan turned and smiled at her, a little twisted smile. But he didn't say anything. Instead, he grabbed a long match from its box, struck it, and lit the paper inside the stove. He closed the door of the stove and stood.

In truth, he hated peach, too. He hated the way the bedroom looked but he couldn't admit it. He wanted to say, "I hate peach, too. Let's change it." He wanted to laugh about their rotten peach bedroom, write graffiti all over it, cover their bodies with paint, and slam naked into the walls making body prints, and then finally paint over it with some neutral color they could both live with. All he wanted to say was, "I hate peach, too," to admit it, but instead, he reached down somewhere rotten and said, "Just live with it. Why can't you just live with things? You think a new color in the bedroom is really going to make a difference in your life?"

She recoiled. "I hate you," she said and ran into the peach bedroom and slammed the door.

Dan followed her inside. She was crumpled on the bed, crying into the pillow. He couldn't understand why she was crying. He grabbed the empty bottle of the Great Doctor Kilmer's Swamp Root Kidney Liver Bladder Cure. He grabbed it because it was hers and she had given it to him. He turned and started out the room with the bottle in his hand.

"Where are you going?"

"To the ocean. I'm going to throw this bottle in the ocean."

She laughed at him. "There is no ocean. Don't be a fool."

"I'll find one," he said. And he meant it. He left the house with nothing but the bottle, intending to drive a thousand miles to the nearest ocean.

"You think I care about that stupid bottle," she screamed after him from the front door. The school bus had just stopped at the end of their street and the children looked up at her and then away.

Dan stood on the porch looking at the car. He didn't want to go. How did he get here? he wondered. A moment before, he was ready to drive to the ocean, but now all he wanted was to surrender to his love for her.

Instead, he said in a voice that was not his, "I am Lazarus. I have lain in the desert. The sun has bleached my bones and I have risen with new flesh and I have returned to the valley and its people."

He felt the struggle inside him. He simply wanted to be who he was. He wanted for them to be who they were together, but there was something different going on, something confused and desperate.

The something inside him was telling him what to say. It wanted him to say to Molly, "Let me minister to you, child. Let's wang dang doodle all night long. Let's roll in God's mercy and man's hatred like dogs reveling in a dead animal's scent. Make me hate myself, child. Make me hate you. And together let us enter the kingdom of loathing for our worldly flesh without end."

But he fought it off. He fought it back. He wasn't going to say those things to Molly. He didn't hate himself. He didn't hate Molly.

Instead, he turned to her meekly and said, "Um . . . ." He offered her the empty bottle and brushed his hair from his eyes.

She glared at him, chin out. That was an awful thing he had said. She never complained, and there were things, O Lord, she could have complained about. Peach was the least of it. She wanted to punish him for it. But she was merciful. She took the bottle and put it to her lips as though it weren't empty. She took a draught and smacked her lips. "That's powerful medicine." And she handed the empty bottle back to him.

He took a sip from the empty bottle, too, and felt refreshed.

"I could live with peach," she said.

They went back inside and lay together like husband and wife, though they were not. They had spoken of marriage, but neither saw the need, not after so long.

As they lay in each other's arms, they heard something thud and then smash against the wall.

They sat up and Molly flicked on the bedside light. The bottle of Dr. Kilmer's medicine lay smashed at the base of the wall nearest the door. A thick black liquid oozed around it.

"Hey, I liked that bottle," yelled Dan.

"Idolaters! Fornicators!" a voice yelled and the lava lamp again hovered above their bed.

"Jesus," Molly said in surprise.

"Come to Jesus," the voice said.

"Leave us alone," said Dan. "Leave us in peace."

The thing quivered as though it were laughing and it yelled at them ferociously, though neither could make out exactly what it was saying. It sounded like, "The dogs of heathen shall eat nothing but meat by-products!"

"I could live with a ghost or I could live with a preacher," Dan said, rising up in bed. "But I'd rather live with a ghost than a preacher. I definitely can't take living with a combination of the two." He stood with the sheet around him, embarrassed by his nakedness. He swatted at the lava lamp, but it spun around him and screamed "Abomination! Blasphemers!" And then it sounded garbled again. "And there will be no motion sickness among you!"

"Maybe we could call the Catholic church," Molly said.

Dan sat down again. "It's a Baptist preacher, Molly. I can tell. Catholics aren't going to get involved."

Molly, who was feeling conciliatory, and had room in her heart for even such an apparition, felt a need to compromise. "Maybe we could share the house. You could preach to us on Sunday mornings."

"Lovely to look at, nice to hold," the apparition said in its deep preacher's voice. "But if you break God's covenant, consider it sold!"

"Why aren't you in heaven if you're such a good preacher?" Molly screamed.

The apparition blinked out again.

Over in the corner, a luminescent mist began to rise from Dr. Kilmer's Swamp Root medicine jar. It swirled into a gossamer vortex and slowly filled out until it took the shape of a man, a shimmering reflection on water, the silhouette behind a two-way mirror. The man looked to be in his forties. His hair was red and thin and slicked down across his wide skull. His face was pasty and pocked, his cheeks full, and he wore a cold grin. He was naked except for a pair of leopard-spot bikini briefs. His flesh hung down in little terraces like a garden on a mountain slope.

"He doesn't look like a preacher to me." Molly said.

The apparition reached out its hand toward Dan and Molly. He wasn't smiling anymore. He seemed to be sweating profusely like he'd just been doing something strenuous. "Men's evil manners live in brass; their virtues we write in water."

"We're going to have to move, Dan," Molly said.

"No," he said. "We can ride him out."

"He's going to ruin everything between us," she said. "He makes me feel . . ."

"I know," said Dan. She didn't need to finish her sentence. She really didn't even need to talk at all. "He makes me feel the same."

The next day they started packing. They would sell their house at a loss. You had to stay in a house at least three years to realize a profit. And both were basically good, honest people, so when they filled out the seller's questionnaire, they'd have to put down "Haunted by ghost of fundamentalist minister—if you believe in such things." They could move into a condo, Dan thought. That's all they'd be able to afford, and where would they store all their possessions?

"Who needs possessions?" Molly said.

When they left the house to stay in a motel, they heard the ghost behind them, still preaching. He never gave up. They might have listened if he'd had a different way and if he didn't look and act so ridiculous. "Are you afraid for your immortal souls?" the ghost screamed. Dan and Molly made their way down the walkway, not looking back and never to return. They held hands tightly, each ready to rescue the other from earthly and unearthly torments, and fought against the petty feelings in their chests and stomachs, rising.

Devotion

Ray constantly tamped down his self-doubts and dissatisfactions, but they kept reaching up like zombies out of the grave. And what was there to be dissatisfied about? He owned a moderately successful restaurant, Raisin D'etre (serving raisin- and grape-inspired dishes) on Railroad Avenue in Bellingham, frequented by artist types and professors and students from Western Washington University.

There were people he knew who would die to be him, but this did not help. What helped was a light box—he suffered from Seasonal Affective Disorder—a prescription of Zoloft, and once-a-week visits to a therapist in Seattle. These helped enormously. But what helped the most was living life unselfishly, trying to give back to the community in which he lived. He and his wife Bridget, who worked as a realtor, donated their time and leftovers from the restaurant to a soup kitchen. He also allowed local artists to display their work on the walls of his restaurant, free of charge. Was this sufficient? He didn't know. Sometimes, he felt he wasn't being unselfish enough and this added to his sense of overall dissatisfaction. Sometimes, he wondered what would happen if he died on some uneventful day, as he knew he would someday, overcome with petty worries about broken plumbing, or debt, or the waiter he knew he had to fire. In an instant, these worries would mean nothing. They would evaporate on his death. The debt would be paid by Bridget or it wouldn't. The plumbing would be fixed eventually. The waiter would continue to work there after new management took over, or he'd find another job, completely unaware that his old boss had intended to fire him, but had suffered a fatal heart attack instead from worry over it. And the boss? A spirit wandering in the afterlife, chasing his dissatisfaction, mourning everything in life he'd forgotten to be thankful for.

The waiter he had to fire was a guy his own age or older named Harlan. Eerily contented, Harlan didn't seem to have a care, or motivation, or drive. That was unfair perhaps. He had some drive, but it was mostly reverse. He could hardly remember who had ordered what, and sometimes seemed to forget entirely that he was at work. Sometimes, Ray would step into the kitchen and there would be Harlan, smiling and shaking his head, looking up at the ceiling as though he saw an angel floating there. Ray hated firing anyone—the worry over it manifested itself physically. His nose would break out in a bright red rash and his skin would start peeling. It happened almost instantaneously whenever he stressed out. What made it worse was that Harlan was one of the artists whose work was displayed in the restaurant. Harlan was a photographer, and his photography was only marginally better than his waiting skills. In the eleven months his photographs had been displayed at the restaurant, not one had sold. They weren't bad, but they weren't good. They were photos of human forms surrounded by floating fruits and vegetables. Harlan explained that he had his subjects lie nude on a double-layered Plexiglas table. The bottom pane held the fruits and vegetables. The model lay on top. There was nothing particularly awe-inspiring or disturbing or original about the series. It seemed simply a waste of fruits, vegetables, and nude bodies.

Harlan sat at a booth counting his tips from a plastic cup when Ray strode into the restaurant on the day he decided to fire the waiter. Harlan seemed a cross between an ape—thick arms and legs, simian-shaped head—and the Italian artist Raphael as seen in a painting Ray had seen at the Louvre with Bridget. Ray had touched Harlan's shoulder in nearly the same manner as depicted in the painting of Raphael and his friend, and when Harlan turned to see who it was, the painting flashed into Ray's mind. But this was a modern version of the painting: Portrait of the Waiter Counting Out His Tips Before His Boss Fires Him.

Harlan offered him the seat across from him and smiled sadly.

"What's wrong?" Ray asked.

"I've been thinking," Harlan said, smoothing a dollar bill flat with the palm of his hand. "I need more time for my work, to devote myself to it, and this job, as kind as you've been to me, is a distraction. Besides, I'm not a very good waiter if you haven't noticed." He looked up at Ray and smiled broadly with yellowed teeth. "I'm going to have to give two weeks' notice." He looked in the direction of the wall where his photos hung.

"Two weeks, huh?" Ray said.

"It could be longer if you need me. It's just that . . . well, my wife told me she wanted a divorce a week ago and I'm kind of off-balance."

Off-balance? That's all the guy felt? No wonder he was getting a divorce. If Bridget ever left him . . . sometimes, he imagined it. All because of his selfishness. This was one of his chief worries, that he did not love his wife sufficiently. Devotion is easy when you're young and new at love, but even the most loving couples he knew became little more than business partners after a few years. He didn't buy her flowers anymore except on Valentine's Day. He only bought her presents for her birthday and at Christmas. Everything was too routine. Sure, he'd die for her, stop a terrorist's bullet, but it's on the level of the everyday that the quality of one's devotion is proven.

Ray made a cluck of sympathy. "Oh man, I'm sorry. No, we'll get by."

Ray might have relaxed just then, might have gone limp with relief and gratitude toward God and fate that he had been spared the task of firing Harlan. Instead, he felt suddenly awash in pity. How was it that self-recognition only went so deep, stopping short of one's fatal flaw? Harlan knew he was a bad waiter, but had no inkling that he was also a bad artist. He was going to quit his paying job so he could devote himself to art, which quite obviously he couldn't make a living doing. And going through a divorce on top of it? He'd be begging in the streets in a month tops. What was it about art that so deluded people into thinking they were good when they obviously weren't? At least as a waiter he wouldn't starve. Why devote yourself to anything unless you were good at it? That's why he'd quit painting years ago, around the time he'd met Bridget in Chicago. He had been only good, not great, and not being great was unbearable to him. The world didn't need any more good artists anyway, but it could always use another good restaurant.

"Are you sure you want to do this?" Ray asked Harlan. "Have you thought this over fully? You can always come back if you need to. Your job will be waiting."

"You're a generous, unselfish man," Harlan said, reaching across the table and touching Ray's hand. "I hope you know that."

Ray sat up in the booth. He wanted to shout Yes! Bingo! You listening, God? You hear that? A generous (Rah Rah!) unselfish (Can you say it a little louder?) man (Now put it all together and what do you get?!). But he couldn't give in to such impulses, of course, so he just smiled and said, "A little tea and sympathy, my man. It costs nothing. Part of being human."

You couldn't just tell someone they stink, but that's what Ray wanted to tell Harlan. "Your art is terrible. I'm saying this as a friend. I know this is a dream of yours, but you have no talent and without talent there's no way you'll ever realize your dream. But that's okay. You can still live a fruitful (no pun intended), productive life." That's what he wanted to say, but of course he'd never say it because he was not a cruel person, and only cruel people dashed the dreams of others. Or perhaps they were the kindest, but regardless, Ray was not one of them.

"I'll be okay," Harlan said, patting Ray's hand as though *he* needed comfort.

"You're still going to display your photographs here, I hope," Ray said. Why had he said that? He certainly didn't want them anywhere near his restaurant. The only thing that made them bearable was that the bodies were nice bodies, not corpulent, but nubile. And they were all in good taste. Maybe a stray pubic hair here and there, but no genitalia, just breasts, buttocks, lithe arms and legs, taut abs. The fruit was ripe, too.

"I hadn't thought about that," Harlan said. "To be honest, I'm not really that attached to them. Why don't you take them with my compliments? At least I'll know they've gone to a good home."

This was worse than firing the guy, Ray thought. No wonder he wasn't going anywhere as an artist. How could anyone else be "attached" to your work if you weren't? And why quit your job if you cared so little about your own work?

"That's very generous," Ray said, about to add, "But I can't accept them," when he looked up to see Bridget walking into the restaurant. For some reason, he ducked his head as though he were about to be caught in some life-altering lie. He wasn't sure if Bridget had spotted him. She bounded to the water jar, took a red plastic glass, and filled it. Then she drank deeply as though she had been in the scorching heat for hours. But outside, the sky was overcast and a drizzle was blowing against the windows. Things like the weather never seemed to bother Bridget. It was a corny thought, but she really did seem to carry the sun with her. She moved him to say stupidly sincere things even after eighteen years. Last night, he had told her that after he died, he promised he wouldn't haunt her. "Ssshh," she'd said and laughed. "Only you know how to be simultaneously touching and creepy."

The way she looked out the window of the restaurant toward the diffused light reminded him of a painting he had once seen. It bumped around the palace of his mind, tripping over recipes and To Do lists: the light coming in from the window, the blue dress, white bonnet, the map on the wall. With one hand, she held the window. With the other, she held the jug. She regarded the window as though she weren't looking out but studying the design on it or a smudge.

Bridget seemed lost in thought. There had been a smile on her lips after she drank her water, but now she looked vaguely troubled. She put her glass in the bus tray near the garbage cans and left the restaurant again, returning moments later with a tray of lamb's ears. She seemed now to notice Ray and her expression brightened.

Inexplicably, she carried the tray of lamb's ears to the table, set it down, and broke off a leaf from one of the plants. By way of hello, she put a leaf under Ray's nose and said, "Sniff." So he sniffed. "What does it smell like?"

"Sweet," Ray said.

Although she didn't know Harlan (maybe she'd seen him once or twice waiting tables), she placed the leaf under his nose.

"Sniff," she said, and he sniffed.

"What does it smell like?"

"7-Up," he said.

She raised her hand and he slapped it. Ray simply stared at her, awed. What made her so comfortable in the world?

"7-Up," she said. "Isn't it marvelous? It's a special kind of lamb's ear. Most don't have any smell at all. Oh, did I interrupt something? Should I take my lamb's ears and skedaddle, because I'm good at that, you know. I can skedaddle with the best of them."

"Wow," Harlan said, staring at her. Then he looked at Ray. "Man, I hope you appreciate this woman."

Yes, he appreciated her. This wasn't the first time he had been told to appreciate her. On the street, he had been stopped more than once and accosted by strange men who looked homeless. Each told him through words or gestures how fortunate he was to have Bridget. Once in Montreal, once in San Francisco, and once at an airport (LAX? O'Hare? DFW?) years ago.

Ray introduced Harlan to Bridget (I've seen you around. You, too), and before long, they were discussing lamb's ears and other perennials. Harlan asked Bridget if she'd consider posing amidst the lamb's ears at his studio. He thought this was just the touch his photos needed. "Those are my photos," he said, pointing to the wall above the heads of diners in their various booths, eating couscous, stuffed grape leaves, kugel, strudels.

"Those are yours?" she said. Ray peered into her eyes, trying to discern the faintest glimmer of abject horror. "I admire them every time I come in here."

Harlan smiled and picked up the lamb's ear and sniffed it again as though it smelled of ambrosia, not 7-Up. Inwardly, Ray groaned. A studio.

Ray studied his wife's face to see if she wore a mask of sincerity or if she really believed his work was good. If his work was so good, why didn't anyone buy it? Why was he a waiter in a mid-priced restaurant in Bellingham, Washington at the age of forty-five?

"Harlan wants to give them to us," he said.

"Oh you can't," she said and looked at Ray as though she'd just been offered the keys to a new Jaguar.

"That's what I was trying to tell him," said Ray.

"Why don't you and Ray come to my place for dinner this weekend?" Harlan said. "I'd like the chance to matte the photos and frame them better. I did a bit of a rush job for the wall at the restaurant. And I have some other works I'd like to show you since you're both art lovers." Bridget was delighted, but Ray imagined spaghetti with meat sauce from a jar, pre-buttered garlic bread you heat in the oven, maybe packaged Caesar salad. Unbearable. Was that whiny and ungrateful? Yes, he knew it was. But hadn't he earned just a little ingratitude? He was nothing if not generous. He helped strangers, did random acts of kindness. He rescued fallen birds. He saved a woman's life once with the Heimlich. He sent money to children in Nicaragua every month.

In a past life, as one says when one marvels at the unfathomable twists and turns of one's existence, Ray and Bridget had both been young painters at the School of the Art Institute in Chicago. Prior to that, Bridget had briefly been a novitiate. They'd met two years after she'd left her order—he'd never known her when she thought she wanted to be a nun. They were both twenty-five, born days apart in fact, but worlds away. Bridget had been born in Ireland and moved to Chicago when she was twelve, but had completely lost her Irish accent. Ray had been fascinated by her former career path—to him, a Jewish kid from Marin County, being involved with a nun was like romancing a mermaid, illogical, mythical, practically impossible, but so intriguing as to make him mad with lust. He was full of questions. What made her leave?

"The better question," she said, "would be what made me go into the order in the first place, and the answer to that would be my parents. And that answer should take care of all your other questions, too."

She confessed to him one night that she wasn't really interested in pursuing art either. She'd seen it simply as something to do to wean herself from her old life, a hobby. Ray had been aghast, but he'd said nothing. She was someone with real talent, so much talent in fact that it made him doubt his own. She'd done a whole series of paintings that he adored, depicting lovers taking leave of one another. In each painting, one lover was disproportionate to the other. Sometimes, an arm would be distended as in a funhouse mirror, in another, a woman's head or a man's stomach or a woman's breasts. His favorite showed a crying woman leaving a man's apartment, the man at the door bidding her to leave, the woman trying to go, but her arm stretching and stretching, unable to let go. He asked her who or what she had based the paintings on. "Nothing really," she said. He knew she was lying, but she refused to say more.

He had a task ahead of him. He would have to convince her of her worth as an artist. Someday they'd look back on this moment when he'd shown her her own heart, that the world would be an empty place without her talent. He imagined the two of them at a Manhattan art dealer's party twenty years hence, him retelling the story of how he persuaded her to stay on the right path. It was a pleasant moment, and he fell asleep imagining it.

One day and four hours short of twenty years later, Ray sat not in an apartment in SoHo, but in a car on a lovely coastal road, Chuckanut Drive, headed for dinner at a former employee's place. In a sense, he had fallen asleep twenty years earlier, dreamed a pleasant dream, and awakened in someone else's world, someone else's body. It was not a horrible fate, just different from what he had imagined once.

It puzzled Ray to be driving this particular road in his gold-colored Subaru on this particular evening because they were on their way to the dreaded dinner with Harlan. The wealthy live here: once-famous members of defunct bands, best-selling authors, professionals, and the lucky professor or two from the university who bought back in the '60s, prior to the great Californian migration north.

The road dipped around a creek and entered a damp hanging darkness of cedars and forlorn madrones peeling orange bark, then hugged the cliffs over the bay lined with aging white barriers peeling paint. There was something simultaneously elegant and decrepit about the barriers. They had a quaintness that appealed to him—in an antique store on the Olympic Peninsula, he'd once seen a print from the '30s that depicted this same stretch of

Chuckanut with the same barriers, but white and new. He hadn't bought the print because it seemed too expensive for what it was—$75—and it was made by some unknown artist, and anyway, he didn't live on Chuckanut so what was the point?

Not far beyond the barriers, Ray turned left per his instructions from Harlan, up a dirt and gravel road that led up Chuckanut Mountain. They followed the road a quarter of a mile past gates and no-trespassing signs and glimpses of cedar-shingled houses through the trees, some with boats in the driveway. The gates were the type to keep nothing out but vehicles, not much more than poles across the road. The car kicked up gravel as it climbed ever steeper. "Must be hard to drive in the winter," Ray said to Bridget.

"I wouldn't mind," she said.

Sometimes Ray suspected he might already be dead, and that the life he was living had been lived many times before. Sometimes he felt his fate was to relive through eternity, to make the same mistakes over and over without ever once getting wiser. It wasn't déjà vu, because déjà vu is when one feels something familiar in the unfamiliar. No, everything felt as though he were living it for the first time, but sometimes he only suspected he wasn't. And wouldn't that be a cruel fate, to be locked in unalterably to the same life, the same choices with the same results—with only the faintest inkling or suspicion that it had been misspent. Not that his life was so bad, but what did it amount to finally? Raisins? This was a question for his therapist, or maybe a reason to increase the dosage of Zoloft, or to stick his head further into the light box. This was a reason not to drive further up this dark road—yes, there would be stunning views on top and a story, but he didn't necessarily want to see those views or hear that story.

The car climbed up the steepest fork in the dirt road until the house Harlan lived in came into view. The house sat perched near a rock outcropping from which one could see Orcas Island and other smaller islands in the San Juans. The sun reflected off the water almost explosively amid a flotilla of sails, a perfect melding of the man-made and natural worlds. From this vantage point, one could see no other house, nor road. Ray knew that it wasn't always sunny up here, but it was sunny now, and the breeze blew a fragrant crisp air that had not even a hint of rain, or moss, or decaying leaves. The two left their car silently, closing their doors as though trying not to surprise some remarkable creature they had stopped for.

Ray had picked up a bottle of cheap Shiraz for Harlan, but suddenly it seemed inadequate. He went back to the car and swapped the Shiraz for a pricey bottle of Canoe Ridge Merlot that he'd picked up for himself.

"Do you think he rents?" Ray asked Bridget.

"What kind of rent could he pay for this?"

"He can't own it," he said. "How could he afford this?"

"Family money, I guess."

"Maybe this isn't the right address," he said. "He never mentioned any of this. He must be house-sitting. Probably a place to stay while he's sorting through his divorce."

"Either that or . . ." She didn't finish her thought.

Ray saw from Bridget's expression that she was as hypnotized by the spot as he. The house had a deck that stretched all the way around. The boards were clean, not covered with moss or weathered, but seemed to have been pressure-washed lately or were new. The cedar roof was the same: clean and solid, no hint of warping or rot. The pathway to the front door was lined with hostas and bleeding hearts, among them a few bait traps with dead slugs floating. But other than this hint that there was toil involved to maintain such beauty, the house seemed like some enchanted creation. On the side were colorful ceramic tiles from Central or South America (to offset those dreary Northwest days, Ray guessed), strawberry pots brimming with strawberries sunning near the edge of the outcropping, and elaborate ceramic pots in the shapes of animals, cast about at odd angles, like the refuse of some storied city, some Babylon. Pots of fuchsias cascaded from the eaves along the deck, and hummingbird feeders with red nectar nestled among the pots. A water garden with reeds and irises rippled between the edge of the driveway and the perennial border along the house. Perfect water lilies breathed green in the middle of the pond and sunken eyes peered from the edges of the pool. A sculpture made of junk, welded metals and what looked like a washing machine door, was the yard's central eccentricity, announcing that this was the house of an artist or someone who fancied himself one at least.

It's one thing to think that someone else is a charity case and quite another to feel like the charity case instead. It made Ray feel cheated. He had thought the guy was probably living in a sinkhole with sheetrock. Ray had been prepared to write an elabo-rately high check for Harlan's photos. He had planned to pay him two hundred dollars for the set when they weren't worth a penny. But now that seemed insulting.

Ray and Bridget stood near the pond, each trying to take in their surroundings. The door to the house opened and Harlan stood there, Harlan the failed waiter, the pretentious artist, a Red Hook beer in his hand. Ray felt somehow reassured by the sight of Harlan's potbelly and unruly hair.

The house inside was less wondrous than it appeared outward-ly. Usually, one experiences the opposite effect—an unassuming house from the outside unfolding to reveal a sprawling multilevel mansion inside. But Harlan's house seemed cramped and clut-tered inside, filled with file boxes and folders strewn among over-stuffed pillows. Paintings hung on every available space, some of the oddest paintings Ray had ever seen. The series should have been titled *Amoebic Dysentery Series #12*. The paintings were monochromatic and varied little. Each featured explosive blobs, hideous things. Some of the blobs looked like they were shitting. Others bled profusely. Others made love or ejaculated alone.

God, was this what the guy did when he ran out of money for Plexiglas? But canvas was expensive. And the frames alone were probably worth fifty bucks apiece, maybe more. And what was Harlan doing painting in a mode that had petered out forty years ago? There were probably two hundred of these monstrosi-ties, some hanging, some leaning against the walls. Almost every available space supported a monochromatic bleeding blob. Ray wanted to run back outside, but Bridget had already taken off her shoes and Ray gave the bottle of wine wordlessly to Harlan as though handing over his wallet to a bandit.

"Sorry for the clutter," he said. "I'm doing a little organizing. Have any trouble finding the place?"

"I'll have a Red Hook," Ray said.

"Oh, sure," Harlan said, momentarily befuddled. "Sorry, I forgot to ask."

"Ray," Bridget whispered when Harlan had gone to the kitchen. "He's not your waiter here!"

"I thought he asked us what we wanted to drink."

"He asked us if we had any trouble finding the place, and you said, 'I'll have a Red Hook' as though you were standing at a crowded bar . . ." She shook her head and started attacking his nose with her fingers, ripping dead skin in diaphanous pieces. "Okay, why are you suddenly red and peeling?" she asked as though he could help it.

"My wife is yelling at me."

"I'm not yelling. I'm whispering in a mortified tone. That's no reason to turn into Rudolph."

He batted away her hand and she pursed her lips at him in exaggerated petulance. Ray turned away to get a view of something that wouldn't aggravate him. But aggravation sprouted like mushrooms in the wet cedar forests. On the one hand, the blobs, and over by the front door, the photos that had previously hung in his restaurant, now matted and reframed. He had to admit the frames looked pretty nice. If worse came to worst, he could stick some family photos in them.

Soon, Harlan reappeared with a Red Hook and a glass of Sauvignon Blanc, passing them with a wry smile and an élan that belied his appearance. Certainly, in this surrounding, he seemed more confident, one might even say "suave," than he ever seemed capable of at the restaurant. If he'd always had this bearing, a kind of stage presence that the best wait staff summoned, then Ray never would have thought of firing him.

Harlan led them onto the deck past the framed amoebas. Ray wondered what you'd call a group of amoebas? A flock? A murder? A bevy? Maybe a slide. Ray stumbled and kicked one of the frames. Harlan gasped, bent down, and rubbed a thumb across the frame, made of a simple black wood. He worried at it the way a parent might rub chocolate from a toddler's face and said what a parent might say afterward. "There. Good as new!" Then he straightened the painting against the wall and stood, smiled, and led them outside.

It occurred to Ray that these paintings belonged to Harlan's ex-wife, that this was what was meant by "a little organizing." Ray was in the painful process of dismantling his life with her piece by piece. First the artwork would go, then the house would be sold to strangers, then only the faintest memory of the view they had once shared. Ray swigged his beer. The guy was a devoted husband. You had to give him that. He hadn't even bothered to hang any of his own photos on the walls, but had saved every bit of space for her.

Harlan had a salmon grilling and fresh vegetables: squash and peppers and sweet onions.

"So tell us the story of those marvelous paintings, this house, this view," Bridget said, jumping right in as she always did. A kind of psychic alarm went off in Ray's head whenever he was about to feel supremely dissatisfied with his life. Firefighters rushed in with hoses, which they promptly turned on him, dashing him against the walls of his own envy. He knew that no good could come of this evening, that on some awful level he wished Harlan ill, not good, and he was a smart-enough person to recognize this as an ignoble thing. If he heard stories tonight, he wanted them to be of divorce and suffering, of a happy life ruined by self-absorption and selfish decisions. Who really wanted to share in their neighbor's happiness? No one he knew except Bridget, a woman who overflowed with sincerity and empathy, sometimes so much that Ray felt dizzy and nauseated.

He took a sip of his beer and looked at the fish sizzle. "The story of the view," he said. "It goes back to Genesis. What was it? The third day? After God created Orcas Island, he saw that it was good, so he created the view of it."

Harlan looked at him as though he'd just stepped out of a giant scallop shell. Bridget shoved her hand holding an empty wine glass into his stomach so hard he grunted. "You'll have to get me a lot drunker to find you funny. Get me another glass, okay?"

When Ray returned from the kitchen with his wife's wine, they were in the middle of a conversation. "The person I met was miserable," Harlan said. "Bitter and he lived in a world of darkness."

Ray stopped at the threshold, suspecting for a moment they were talking about him.

"Harlan was telling me about the man who painted all of the works inside. He was someone he once worked for."

"That's how it started out at least," said Harlan. "Here, the fish is done. I grew up in the South—that's why we cover everything with breading, to hide how overcooked it is. But I like things a little blackened when I grill, don't you?"

"I'm sure it will all taste just fine." said Bridget. "It looks delicious."

And it *was* delicious, so good in fact that Harlan was tempted to ask the recipe for the delicate cream sauce Harlan served over the salmon. The vegetables, too, had been grilled and seasoned so perfectly that Ray allowed each slice of zucchini, each pepper and tomato, to take a place of honor in his mouth alone and unharried. But even if the vegetables had been immolated to the point where one would need DNA testing to tell what they were, and the salmon had had the consistency and taste of string cheese, Ray still would have enjoyed his meal. A good wine will wash almost anything down, including a career, which is apparently what had happened to the man who had painted the canvases that crammed the walls of the dining room where they ate, the bathroom where Harlan showered, shaved, etc., every morning, the guest bedroom, the hallways, the library filled with art books, the bedrooms (there were three, only one with an actual bed inside), the living room, the laundry room, and even the heated garage. It took two bottles of wine, the Canoe Ridge that Ray had brought and an equally good South African wine from Harlan's wine cellar (!), for Harlan to finish the story of the paintings.

Harlan had met the artist twenty years ago after he'd returned from graduate school with an unmarketable degree in art history. Artists and writers will generally inure themselves to poverty and obscurity longer than people who are gainfully employed, as long as they believe in their own genius, but art historians, librarians, and archivists depend, for the most part, on the regular paycheck from some sort of institution or another.

Unable to find a university interested in hiring him, Harlan returned to his hometown of Charlotte, North Carolina, where his mother and father, both professors at UNC Charlotte, lived in a drug- and crime-ridden, racially charged part of an otherwise fashionable neighborhood, staking their dreams on gentrification the way some people play the same lotto number every week for twenty years figuring that someday their combination will hit it big. Alas, North Carolina had no lottery, and gentrification teased the block on which Harlan's parents lived, but never went all the way. And Harlan soon saw that he had returned to a set of parents who were strangers to him, who were becoming increasingly embattled and racist in their determination to buy happiness. His father spent half his day lying in wait by the front door to chase off the black kids who dared to steal plums from the tree in his yard. His mother became a hermit, an alarm system junkie whose existence was ruled by electric eyes and security codes.

To get out of the house and away from his demented parents, he did some volunteer work—a friend of his parents knew an elderly man, a locally famous artist, Orville Prescott, who needed some assistance. Orville lived in a stately house in the historic

Dilworth section of Charlotte, in the kind of house and location his parents dreamed of. Orville came from an old moneyed family, and had spent a dissipated youth traveling the world in the '20s and '30s before settling in Provincetown, Massachusetts, where he studied art under the famed Hans Hofmann and was befriended by Edward Hopper and other famous artists of that time and place. For a while, he became a celebrated artist in his own right, exhibiting his paintings in New York and at the Forum 49 gallery, run by the poet Weldon Kees. He lived in Provincetown until the 1960s, when he was called home to Charlotte to take care of his ailing parents. Without a backward glance, he gave up his life in Provincetown and took care of his parents' affairs until they passed away. Afterward, he stayed on in Charlotte through the '60s, '70s, and '80s, sinking into alcohol and obscurity with each passing decade. Over time, cut off from the world he loved and his friends, he gave up painting altogether.

"When I met him," Harlan said, "he was seventy-seven, blind from diabetes and suffering from emphysema on top of it. What he wanted me to do was to read him his mail as well as the many magazines he subscribed to. He had a million subscriptions, and the magazines were in piles around his living room. There was *Art and Architecture, Architectural Digest, Smithsonian, Discover,* the *New Yorker,* the *Atlantic, Harpers,* and *Art in America.* Each pile had a stone on top of it to keep everything in place and in order. We'd go through the table of contents and see if there were any articles he was interested in, and then I'd start to read.

Frequently I'd be interrupted by him correcting me on my pronunciation of a foreign word. I think that was half his enjoyment.

"The only magazine he never had me read from was *Art in America*. The stone never moved from that pile. Once, I asked him why, and he told me it was too painful. He was being exceptionally honest that day. He said that the art world had passed him by and that while he wanted to know what was happening, he couldn't bear the thought of seeing certain artists celebrated whose work he disdained. 'No one writes about me,' he said, 'nor should they, I suppose.'

"'You've been written about before,' I told him.

"'Most of it was rubbish, but there was one intelligent piece that traced the idea of purity in my work and the work of Mondrian.'

"'That was me,' I said. 'I wrote that article.'"

Ray and Bridget had finished eating their dinners., and Ray stood from the dinner table to clear his plate, but Harlan waved him to sit. "No, no leave it. I'll get it later."

"So what was his reaction?" Ray asked.

"I can't imagine that," Bridget said. "You never said a word to him before this?"

"I had had every intention of telling him when the time was right that I'd written about him, that I loved his work. But after the first day, when I saw that his work didn't seem to matter to him anymore, I decided to say nothing. I thought that it might depress him even more. You know, the nineteenth-century French poet Rimbaud stopped writing when he was nineteen years old. He never wrote another poem after that. He died a gun runner and slave trader in North Africa—imagine what he would have said in middle age if you'd asked him about his poetry?"

"*Sacré bleu?*" Bridget asked, wearing her coy little I-still-re-member-my-twelfth-grade-French smile.

Harlan laughed. "Probably. Yes, he would have said '*sacré bleu*' and then he would have spat on you. When you give up something you once loved, you don't want it brought up again. That's why it's so hard for people who've been through a divorce to remain friends."

The divorce. Yes, Ray wanted to ask him about that, and was about to say something when Harlan launched back into his story.

"After that, our relationship changed. He was no longer interested in me reading his mail and magazines, but wanted my views on art and especially his art. He asked me if I would help him catalogue his paintings. He came to depend on me. I was his hope. He said he knew he'd never get any recognition in his lifetime, but maybe afterward his work would be valued. You know, it takes only one person really, and Orville thought I was that person, and I thought so, too, because his work . . . I came to live in it. Orville died two years after we met, and in that time I was able to achieve a lot. I catalogued his work. I wrote letters and articles. Soon, his paintings were being shown in the better galleries in New York, Chicago, and San Francisco. All it took was some effort on my part. It was obvious he was an important artist, just overlooked."

"I hope he appreciated what you did for him," Bridget said.

"Not that any of this made him happy. It didn't. If anything, he seemed more miserable the more recognition he received. It was never enough. 'Tell me I'm amazing,' he told me the day before his death.

"'Orville,' I said. 'I could, but what difference would it make to you?'

"'None,' he admitted. 'I'd think you were lying to make me happy.'

"It's been eighteen years since he died. He made me his executor and I inherited all his paintings, all of these." Harlan swept his hand over and behind him. Then he reached for the bottle of South African wine. There was only a drop left. But Harlan drank it. "That's why I took a job as a waiter. I needed to find a way back into a world that didn't involve Orville Prescott. I mean, I'm grateful to him. I owe him a lot. This house, my livelihood. MoMA just bought two of his paintings. He's much more of a figure now than he ever was in his life." Harlan raised his glass to the ceiling. "You're amazing, Orville! You're friggin' amazing."

"So what's going to happen now?" Ray asked quietly.

"Now?" Harlan said.

"Will the collection be split between you and your wife? And the house . . ."

"My wife?" Harlan said.

"You told me your wife had told you she wanted a divorce."

"Yes, that's true, but we don't live together. She lives in Charlotte. She's lived there for the past twenty years. We were married a year after grad school, right after I started helping Orville. It didn't work out from the start, but we never bothered to divorce. At first, I thought it would hurt her too much and then, after a while, it just seemed unimportant. Most of the time, I forgot I was still married. Then, last week she called and said she wanted a divorce. I know it's strange, but it kind of threw me. It felt almost as though we'd actually been married in more than just name for all those years, and I think a part of me mourned the loss."

Bridget looked upset. "So, why did you waste your time with Orville?" she asked.

"He was a brilliant man, and his art deserved attention."

"But was he worth it?"

"I think so. Look around you."

"It just troubles me," Bridget said as they drove carefully down the darkened drive of Harlan's house. Ray didn't say anything for a minute, to see if there would be more, almost as though he hadn't heard her. After eighteen years, he knew her moods. Funny how he could almost read her mind, but not his own. He knew he had to simply listen. It was obvious what troubled her, but he thought she missed the point, that she was being too judgmental, which was unlike her. You could see what Harlan was doing as generous or you could see it as self-serving. She obviously saw Harlan's life as wasted—if he hadn't said that about his wife, he might have earned her admiration. But he'd blown it. In Bridget's book, you didn't stay married to someone for twenty years simply because you forgot to divorce them.

"Don't you think it's parasitic ultimately?"

"Parasitic?" he said. "He's living for someone else, not himself. I wish I had half his devotion."

"Ray, you do all these good things. I wish you could see that. You're a generous, unselfish man."

"I am?" he asked. She looked at him in the darkened car and patted his cheek.

"You work in a soup kitchen. You give your extra food to the Whatcom Food Bank. You treat your employees well."

He waited. He hoped she was going to say something more. No one had ever told him he was amazing. He thought it would feel like a surprise party.

But she was amazing, not him. She'd always been amazing. She could have done so much with her life, but had chosen to live a quiet, ordinary existence. She had been an amazing painter. She probably even would have made an amazing nun. "Are you satisfied?" he asked her.

"I'm stuffed," she said. "Why? Are you still hungry?"

"No, I mean, are you satisfied?"

He could barely see her. She had turned to the window. "No," she said in a small voice. And then again, "Mostly not."

He didn't know what to say. Of the possible answers, yes or no, he hadn't expected her in a million years to say "Mostly not." Bewildered and stung, he didn't know what to say. He knew he couldn't ask her anything else about the present, at least not now. He wasn't prepared. What if she answered something else he

didn't expect? But he had to ask something. It had to be less painful than silence. The old questions came back to him.

"Why did you quit?" he asked her.

"Quit what?"

"Painting. You were so talented. Why did you quit?"

She stayed silent for a long time. Finally, as they were nearing
their house, she said, "Remember that series of paintings I did
that you loved so much, the last paintings I did?"

He nodded.

"Remember Paul?" she said finally.

"Who's Paul?" he asked.

"Paul," she said with feeling, as though he had only known one
Paul in his lifetime.

"Paul Binswanger?" he said. He was their teacher, their professor, actually little more than a boy himself. Barely two years
older than they were, but so successful at twenty-seven that he
didn't last long as an instructor at the Art Institute. Within a
year, he was a celebrated artist, his paintings selling in the high
five-figures. "What? He didn't like those paintings?"

"He never saw them," she said.

She didn't have to say more. He recalled the paintings, the
disproportionate lovers, the woman with the arm that wouldn't
let go, and he knew that she and Paul had been lovers and that
Paul had obviously rejected her. Maybe they'd only been together
for a month, maybe for a week, but it didn't matter. He was her
professor and she had admired him. Now she probably knew that
she'd been foolish to turn her back on her work, all that power

she'd given that guy, the power to change her destiny. And it was too late for her now. Of course, many people, Paul undoubtedly included, would say if she gave up that easily, she must not have had it in her in the first place. But that, he knew, was the easy rationalization of a successful and hardy man who needed only the public's approval.

At the first opportunity, he pulled over, made sure no cars were coming from either direction, and cautiously crept back up the way he'd just come.

"Why are you turning around?" she asked.

"He forgot to give me my photos," Ray said. Why Ray wanted those photos now he couldn't say for sure. He was still thinking of Paul, seeing him in front of the classroom expounding so self-confidently all his views on art.

Their golden Subaru swam through the night. Had they been able to see themselves from afar, one or the other might have been reminded of a painting by Paul Klee, titled *The Golden Fish*. In the painting, a bright golden fish swims amid a clutter of dark shapes, oblivious to their sameness. It swims purposefully in the center of these crowded waters, assured and unfearful of where it's headed. Other fish make way, both exalted and humbled by its luminous presence as it lights a path briefly through the mysterious deep. At least, that's what critics had written, but Ray and Bridget might have seen something entirely different.

Dead Silence

May 22nd:

Downey sits in her Barcalounger, a bowl of popcorn beside her, with the TV tuned to the 1962 film *My Geisha*, starring Shirley MacLaine, though it's low, hardly audible. She flips the lever on her chair so that the attached footrest swings up and the back of the chair reclines. "I didn't sign up for this," she says, her signature line, and her audience applauds warmly.

But she did. Her house is in a cul de sac, one of its best features, in a Talk Show subdivision built around the year 5 A.J.D. The talk show neighbors on her right, the Delarges, have had their final season after a disappointing stand in the ratings, and the house is for sale. On the left, *The Simons Show* isn't faring much better.

176

The host and her guests hardly ever speak to one another and the band doesn't even strike up the theme music of *The Simons Show* anymore, it's so demoralized. Downey's own studio band is fronted by her husband, legendary sax man Serge Perkins, who plays with all the greats: Stan Getz, Robert Palmer, Tommy Dorsey, Martha and the Motels, Xavier Cugat, Van Morrison, the Boston Pops, Frédéric Chopin, and Bix Beiderbecke.

Downey's house has a vaulted ceiling over an open floor plan about the size of a small studio. The audience sits in an addition that all the Talk Show houses in the subdivision have, large enough to seat about 120 people on a portable grandstand.

Legendary makeup artist Shu Uemura sits on Downey's couch dressed in a gray Armani suit with emerald cufflinks. Downey has hosted many dead people as guests, including Napoleon, who gave her some basic French lessons and taught her to make beef Wellington, one of her most highly rated episodes ever.

In the beginning, it was something special to book the dead, but all the talk shows do it so it's nothing special anymore, like the first time, back in 2032, when Judgment Day finally rolled around and the dead came back to life. Non-Judgment Day, really. A lot of wailing and teeth-gnashing and repenting for a week while the dead walked around kind of bewildered among the living. And then nothing. No big announcements from God. No choosing sides as in Capture the Flag. No Jesus. No angels. Just a flugelhorn blast heard worldwide and the dead roaming around an already crowded planet. Finally, they left again. For a while. And then they came back in drips and drabs. Dead awhile then alive. Dead awhile then alive. Dead/Alive/Dead/Alive. After a while even miracles become quotidian if repeated often enough. Time didn't end. But it definitely slowed down. By a week. Another week had to be distributed among the months to account for the extra days. A new bewildering epoch in human history had begun: A.J.D. The general consensus was that Someone had fucked up royally but was too proud to admit it.

Downey offers Shu some popcorn, and he reaches for some but she pulls it back. "Ah, faked you out, Shu!" she says and puts up her hand to high-five him, but he just stares at her hand and straightens his tie.

"So, Shu, I know you began your legendary career in 1928."

"No, Downey, that is when I was born."

"Okay, so Shu me! You ever have anyone say that to you? So Shu me?"

"No, never."

"I love Shirley MacLaine," Downey says, her eyes on the TV screen, where Shirley MacLaine, dressed in a stunningly white fur coat, stands next to Yves Montand, who plays her husband in the film, as she gawks at a group of geishas.

"I love Shirley, too," says Shu.

"She gave you your first big break, didn't she, Shu?"

"In a manner of speaking. She was doing a movie called *My Geisha*, which we watch now. I was working as Hollywood beautician then when I got a call from Harvey P. Selznick. He was the first cousin of legendary producer David O. Selznick. I cut Harvey's hair and he liked so when the makeup artist on *My*

Geisha get ill with appendicitis, they call me and I transform Shirley from white Shirley with red hair to Geisha. You can't tell difference between her and real Geisha."

"That must be nice being a legend," Downey says. "Could you make me into a legend?"

"No. Easier to make you into Geisha."

"Could you make me into a Geisha?"

"No. Can't do that either. Why you want to be Geisha anyway? Be proud of what you are. Barcalounge-sitting female talk show host in sweatpants. I have something better for you, Downey. My special Deep Sea Facial Mist. Made from purest source of water in world extracted from deep seas of Japan."

"I bet this is expensive stuff."

"It is. Nothing more pure than Deep Sea Facial Mist. If you apply, it erase all impurities."

"Maybe it will erase my face," she says.

"Maybe," he says.

"That was supposed to be a joke."

"Deep Sea Facial Mist no joke. Very pure."

"I'd like to talk about your death from pneumonia in 2007. I know it's a difficult subject, but . . ."

"Not difficult. In Japan, we don't scare about death like you Americans."

"Your wife and son were with you when you passed?"

"That's right."

"What was that like? Did you see a white light? Did you think of all you had accomplished but how it meant nothing to you now because you hadn't spent enough time with your kids?" She always asks questions like this. Every once in a while she makes the eyes of the dead go watery. She's famous for making the dead tear up, if for nothing else. It's a gift.

Shu Uemura lies on the couch and coughs weakly. Then he sits up again. "That's what it was like. I don't tell you secret formula of Deep Sea Facial Mist. I don't tell you what it like to be dead. Like magician. I don't reveal our secrets."

SWEEPS WEEK, 35 A.J.D.,
The Downey Perkins Show

May 23rd:
Downey chats with the studio audience from her Barcalounger while Serge goes through the audience with a portable mic.

"How many of you have been dead seventy-five years or more?" Downey asks. "A show of hands. A lot of you, eh? A millennium? More? Stand up, yes, you stand up. What's your name?"

"My name is Zafora," says a shy-looking girl about fifteen with dark hair pulled back in a ponytail, and wearing a white dress and sandals.

"And you've been dead . . . ?"

"About 2,500 years. I was a slave girl in Thrace."

"That's in South America somewhere?"

"Around the Balkans, actually."

"Your English is great for a dead . . . Thrace person."

"Thank you, Mistress. I learn from watching your show."

"Well, isn't that something!? Do we have anything for her, Serge?"

"How about a tee shirt?" he says, pulling one from a bag and displaying it. I DIDN'T SIGN UP FOR THIS! is emblazoned in purple script with a drawing of Downey sitting in her Barcalounger. The girl accepts the gift with obvious delight and sits down.

The doorbell rings.

"It's not locked!" Downey shouts.

The door swings wide open and in strides Sunshine Dupree, and the band strikes up the Sunshine Dupree theme, "The Sunny Side of the Street." Sunshine, a woman in her late thirties, dressed in a smart ensemble of a simple blue sundress and straw hat, and a Ferragamo clutch, walks into the living room and pauses—two beats—and flops down on the couch near Downey's Barcalounger.

"Is it cocktail hour yet?"

"It's cocktail hour somewhere, Sunshine," Downey says. "Help yourself to some of that box wine I've got in the fridge. It's from Australia." Sunshine pops up from the couch as though she's about to start an aerobics routine.

"Hey Sunshine," says Serge, leering at Sunshine. "Get me a glass of that wine from Down Under, will you, while you're in the fridge? You know that box wine is pretty good," says Serge to Downey.

Sunshine returns with two glasses of wine and hands one to Serge, who downs his in one gulp. She sits beside Downey, who offers her some popcorn, which Sunshine waves away. "So what brings you to my show, Sunny?"

"I just wanted to tell you and your audience about my new show. The whole show will be broadcast from my car, where I'll be living with my three children after the end of this month when my house is foreclosed. My guests will include my three children plus assorted terrifying strangers and predators. You never know who will drop by. My special musical guest will be AM radio. I would probably kill myself if not for my children. I still might. It can't be that bad, is it?" She looks at the audience.

The men and women in the audience, boys and girls, close their eyes and fold their hands over their chests.

"You're not getting anything out of them," Downey says.

"Anyway," Serge says. "Things will get better. Look at the sunny side!"

Serge and the band strike up "The Sunny Side of the Street" and Downey draws a finger across her throat and sticks out her tongue, corpse-like, then takes a sip of wine while Sunshine stifles a sob.

"So Sunshine, have you brought us any crafts or recipes from your new show to share with the audience?"

"As a matter of fact, I have," she says, setting her glass of wine down on the floor. "They're called Depression Eggs."

"Sounds like my ovaries," says Downey.

"Let's go to the kitchen and prepare them, shall we? Though you don't need a kitchen. You can cook them on your car radiator."

"I'm fine here. You just fix me up some."

Shouts come from outside and the front door opens—Sunshine Dupree's son Petey runs wildly toward his mother, followed by her estranged husband Ray, dressed only in his underwear and wielding a toilet plunger.

"He's going to kill me, Mom," Petey screams as Sunshine wraps her arms around him and faces off with Ray with his toilet plunger raised. "You little shit," he yells, his signature line, as Serge starts up Ray's theme music, "You Little Shit."

"You're on a respectable talk show, you moron," Downey tells him.

"That reminds me," says Sunshine. "Petey thinks the song 'That's Amore' is 'That's a Moron.' Don't you, Petey?" she asks the trembling boy. Petey looks up at her, smiling, and sings "When the moon hits your eye like a big pizza pie, that's a moron."

The audience claps and laughs as Ray lowers his plunger and skulks toward the front door. As he's about to leave, he shakes his plunger and shouts to no one in particular, "You're dead! You're all dead!"

Downey and Sunshine exchange looks. "Damn," Downey mutters. "Great line."

Serge stares at his sax. "I didn't get the music for that one."

SWEEPS WEEK, 35 A.J.D.,
The Downey Perkins Show

May 22nd:

A lot of dead musicians are sitting in tonight with Serge and the band in preparation for the legendary Dean Martin's appearance on *The Downey Perkins Show.* They've spared no expense, done up in white tuxes, the wind section filled out with such legends as Illinois Jacquet, Sonny Rollins, Rahsaan Roland Kirk, Chuck Mangione, Zamfir, Master of the Pan Flute, even Tommy Dorsey and Stan Getz back again, all of them dead for many years but blowing like they can blow themselves alive again for good, like they're blowing in Judgment Day itself, which it is, in a sense, except that it's Sweeps Week, which has supplanted Judgment Day because Judgment Day is over and it was a bust.

They're playing a jazzed-up rendition of "That's Amore," saxes swinging low while the horns swing high and the pan flute swings steady. Even the normally affectless star of the show is snapping her fingers, swaying her head, her bowl of popcorn bouncing precariously on her gargantuan belly. The air thrums with the magic of an orchestra completely in its groove—each note like the bite of a plum or peach ripened with sweet perfection for a moment before the next bite pushes the first into oblivion. The band hasn't sounded that hot since Napoleon made his guest appearance. They're blowin' like Morons in love. They're blowin' for Dino.

From upstairs, a door opens and three men walk down and sit on the couch, one dressed in an Arab headdress and aba, the other two dressed in frumpy wool suits. One, with a bowler hat, has a chubby baby face while the other wears a broader brimmed hat, walks with a limp, and has a walrus mustache and a scowl.

The band stops mid-note.

Downey flips the lever of her Barcalounger and pops up into a sitting position, the popcorn bowl tumbling to the floor. "Where's Dino?" she asks.

"He's not coming," says the man with the bowler. "He send us instead, three famous Italian Americans."

"Famous? I didn't ask for three famous Italian Americans. I asked for Dean Martin."

"I'm Sacco," says the man in the bowler.

"I'm Vanzetti," says the other.

The man in the sheik's outfit stays silent.

"Comedians?" she asks.

"Anarchists," says the man in the bowler.

"Antichrists?" says Serge.

"Anarchists," says Vanzetti.

Downey's face has turned crimson and it looks as though she might fall into one of her famous rages, but her voice comes out weak. "I didn't sign up for this."

"We believe in the violent overthrow of the government. They say we kill a couple of bank guards, but we not do that. They put innocent men to death in the electric chair. Innocent."

"Oh, what does the electric chair feel like? Did you see a white light when you passed?" Downey asks.

Sacco shrugs. Vanzetti doesn't say anything but looks at his feet. The man in the sheik's outfit picks his teeth with a silver pick that glints in the light.

"What about recipes? You have any recipes for our audience?"

"We die in 1917," says the ever-scowling Vanzetti. "The government cook us. We no cook. Our mamas cook. Our wives cook. Our sisters cook. We cook up schemes to overthrow government. You want us to tell you how to make a bomb, we tell you that.

Not a bomb like that idiota Carlo Valdinoci make. He try to plant bomb in U.S. Attorney General's house but it go off in his hands and that's all she write. That idiota."

"Puh. What are you saying?" says Sacco. "Valdinoci was one smart cookie. So he don't know how to make a good bomb, so what? He was a good newspaper editor. You don't even know how to read, Vanzetti. But he was the best editor *Cronaca Sovversiva* ever have."

"I still not talking to him," says Vanzetti. "He's an idiota." He pretends to be juggling a bomb in his hands to the titters of the audience. "Ooh, it gonna blow! Help me, Mama! I don' wanna die!"

"Super," says Downey. "Glad we got that cleared up. So what brings you to my show?"

"This is our first," says Sacco. "No one ask us before."

"I didn't ask you either," says Downey.

"Dino ask us," says Vanzetti. "We're all members of the same Knights of Columbus lodge. He say, 'Do me this favor, boys.'"

"You belong to a Knights of Columbus lodge in the afterlife?" Downey asks.

"Shut up," says Sacco, slapping Vanzetti's hand. "You big mouth. Always getting us in hot water." He turns to Downey, takes off his bowler, and smooths his thin hair. "Forget he say that. We say anymore we have to kill you."

"And your audience," says Vanzetti.

But the audience is already dead, or most of them. They laugh loudly at this. Today, Downey is definitely breaking fire code.

About 250 dead people are crammed in a space meant for 120. But really, what's the big deal about the fire code? So they burn.

"Joke," says Sacco. "Downey, we watch your show all the time."

"You sure you're not two of the Marx Brothers?" Downey asks, which gets a roar of appreciative laughter from the audience. Dead audiences tend to book in blocks, well in advance. Today's audience is made up entirely of the audience of the October 11th, 1956, episode of "You Bet Your Life" with Groucho Marx. Strangers in life, they have found this common bond in death.

"I tell you something, Downey," Vanzetti says, leaning forward, arms on legs. "We anarchists. We don't believe in no rules."

"If you don't believe in rules, why don't you tell me a little more about death?" She looks at the audience. "Clap if you want the antichrist to tell us about death."

There's murmuring in the audience, nervous laughter, but no clapping.

"Anarchist," says Vanzetti. "I met the Antichrist once. He not such a bad guy. What you want to know? I spill all the beans."

"Shut up, I'm tellin' you," says Sacco to Vanzetti. "What you trying to do?" He turns to Downey. "Ask us about our lives. We don't give up any secrets about . . . you know. Okay, I tell you the truth. We did kill those bank guards. We was guilty as hell. There. Scoop of the century. Sacco and Vanzetti Guilty After All."

"Scoop of the century?" says Downey. "If you've got a scoop of ice cream, I'm interested. Otherwise, no one cares. No one's cared for a long, long time. Serge, you ever hear of these guys?"

"I've heard of Dean Martin," he says. Zamfir, Stan Getz, and the others are putting away their instruments, trickling away. "But who's the guy in the Arab get-up?"

"So, Downey," Vanzetti says in that same conspiratorial tone of voice. "The dead say some magic words when they want to be resurrected and say those words when they miss their friends and want to be surrected again."

"Really?" Downey asks. "What are those words?"

Vanzetti leans over and whispers in her ear. A pop and a fizzle and Vanzetti vanishes.

"I didn't get that," she tells Sacco. "Did he say, 'Zohar Magnificat'?" Downey slumps to the floor by her fallen bowl of popcorn.

Sacco punches his bowler and kicks it into the audience. "Damn you, Vanzetti," he says.

"Zohar Magnificat," the audience says in unison as does most of the band, all of them popping away, leaving the man on the couch in the sheik's outfit, still picking his teeth with a silver pick, and Serge Perkins by the now-empty bandstand.

Sacco shakes his head, goes into the empty grandstand to retrieve his punched bowler and puts it on. "Zohar Magnificat," he says and vanishes.

Dead silence.

May 22nd:

Sunshine Dupree sits in a bathing suit in a Jacuzzi alongside Serge Perkins and the horn section of his band. Dean Martin, dressed in a black tux, bends into an old-fashioned mic, smoke curling from the cigarette between his fingers as he croons "Volare."

"Give it up for the immortal Dean Martin," Serge says. "Such an honor, sir!"

Dino gives his famous smile and a nod, waving the hand with the cigarette as though pushing brain waves from his head to the audience.

"How many of you in the audience are among the recently deceased?" Serge asks. "A show of hands.

"Almost the entire audience. With a few notable exceptions, I see. Zafora the Slave Girl from Thrace. Always great to see you and thanks for making the transition from my late wife's show to mine.

"We have a great show for you tonight. Dino will be back for another number later in the show but first, let's give it up for, or should I say, surrender to, my first guest, American Civil War General Zachary Dunright." Serge gets out of the host hot tub and towels off while the band strikes up "The Battle Hymn of the Republic." A middle-aged man with a gray beard in full Union Army dress with a ceremonial sword walks in erectly and takes a seat on the couch, while Serge sits opposite him in a swivel chair. He puts down his sax and grabs a glass of wine from the fridge. "Glad to see you, General. Make yourself at home. Care for any wine?"

"General Grant drinks for all his generals," the General says, "I don't—"

"A little Civil War humor," says Serge, chuckling a courtesy laugh. "So General, what were your last words, if you don't mind repeating them?"

The General clears his throat and points at the audience. "As the Rebels were advancing on us, one of my junior officers expressed concern that I was fully exposed to the enemy on my horse. I looked down at him and laughed. Then I said, 'They couldn't hit an elephant at this dist—'"

"One of the greats," says Serge, pouring himself some more wine and raising the bottle toward the General, who shakes his head again and frowns. "You couldn't have planned better last words. You didn't plan them, did you?"

"Well, no," says the General. "That's what makes them—"

"I bet you still take a lot of ribbing for that," Serge says.

"I'm used to it," says the General. "It's a good—"

"Conversation starter," says Serge. "Obviously."

Gasps from the audience. From offstage, two men push a Barcalounger with the recumbent Downey Perkins, looking exactly as she did in life, down to the bowl of popcorn on her belly.

Sunshine stands up in the hot tub and her signature straw hat falls in the water. Serge nearly drops his wine, but recovers and polishes off the glass before setting it aside. The audience claps wildly. For a long while, Serge doesn't speak and there's no music because he hasn't told the band to play her familiar theme. But then he makes a little wave and they play.

"Hey, Baby. You almost gave me a heart attack," he says when the hooting and clapping have subsided.

"A heart attack would too good for you, two-timer," she says, smiling broadly, playing to the audience with her old flair for the dramatic. "You sax men are all alike. I'm dead five minutes and you hop in the sack with the talk show host next door."

"C'mon, Baby," Serge says. "Don't be that way. I've missed you."

"Like hell. I didn't sign up for this."

"So how's death? I guess it's a part of life, huh?"

She's about to answer, or so it seems, when a flugelhorn sounds a blistering blast, then sputters as though the mouthpiece is full of spit. All heads turn to the horn section, but they're silent. The stage lights flicker and the audience looks up, then down at their shoes as though caught doing something wrong. The lights flicker again and then seem to burn twice as bright. "It's nothing," says Serge. "Go on, Baby. Talk."

Reply All

TO: Poetry Association of the Western Suburbs Listserv
FROM: Lisa Drago-Harse
SUBJECT: Next Meeting
DATE: July 17th

Hi all,

I wanted to confirm that our next meeting will be held in the Sir Francis Drake Room at the Bensenville Hampton Inn on August 3rd. Minutes from our last meeting and an agenda for the next meeting will follow shortly.

Peace and Poetry,
Lisa Drago-Harse
Secretary/PAWS

TO: Poetry Association of the Western Suburbs Listserv
FROM: Michael Stroud
SUBJECT: Re: Next Meeting
DATE: July 17th

Dearest Lisa,

First of all, I *love* your mole and don't find it unsightly in the
least! There is absolutely no reason for you to be ashamed of it
(though it might be a good idea to have it checked out). But please
don't remove it! Heaven forbid, my darling! As I recall, I gave you
considerable pleasure when I sucked and licked it like a nipple.
A nipple it is in size and shape, if not placement. That no one
else knows your mole's position on your body (other than your
benighted husband, poor limp Richard, that Son(net) of a Bitch
as you call him) is more the pity (if Marvell had known such a
mole, he undoubtedly would have added an extra stanza to his
poem). But my coy mistress is not *so* terribly coy as all that, if I
remember correctly (and how could I forget!). You were not at
all what I had expected in bed—not that I had any expectations
at all. When you started massaging my crotch with your foot
underneath the table in the Sir Francis Drake Room, I was at first
shocked. For a moment, I thought perhaps the unseen massager
was none other than our esteemed president, the redoubtable
Darcy McFee (makeup and wardrobe courtesy of Yoda). Is that
terrible of me? I have nothing personal against her, really, except
for her execrable taste in poetry, and the fact that you should be
president, not she. And her breath. And that habit of pulling her

nose when she speaks and that absolutely horrific expression of hers: twee. As in, "I find his poetry just so twee." What does twee mean and why does she keep inflicting it upon us! So imagine my horror when I felt this foot in my crotch and I stared across the table at the two of you—she twitching like a slug that's had salt poured on it and you immobile except for your Mont Blanc pen taking down the minutes. Ah, to think that the taking down of minutes could be such an erotic activity, but in your capable hands, it is. To think that mere hours later, it would be my Mont Blanc you'd grasp so firmly, guiding me into the lyrical book of your body. But initially, I thought the worst, that it was Darcy, not you. My only consolation was the idea that at least I had her on a sexual harassment suit, her being my boss after all at Roosevelt. Another reason I thought it was her and not you was because I know you're married and she isn't and I knew that Richard is a member of our esteemed organization, too (and he was in the room, seated beside you no less!). It was only that sly smile in your eyes that tipped me off. I, too, love the danger that illicit public sex brings, as long as it's kept under the table, so to speak. And yes, maybe someday we can make love on that very same table in the Sir Francis Drake Room, my darling. But I must ask you, sweetheart, where did you learn that amazing trick. I have seen people wiggle their ears before, but never that! What amazing talent and such a pity that this is not something you bring out at parties or poetry readings to awe the dumb masses! Would Darcy find that too twee? I think not! Thinking of you now makes me so hot. I want to nibble you. I want to live in your panties. I want to write a series of odes to you equal in number to every lucky taste bud on my tongue, every nerve ending (no, not endings but beginnings!) on my body that live in rapture of your every pore. No, not poor, but rich. I am rich. I make metaphors of your muscles, of your thighs, of the fecund wetness bursting with your being and effulgence. I must swallow now. I must breathe. I must take my leave, my darling, and go now to relieve myself of my private thoughts of you and you alone.

With undying love and erotic daydreams,

Mikey

P.S. Do you think you could get away for an evening next week? Could you be called away from Richard for an emergency meeting of the Public Relations Committee?

TO: PAWS Listserv
FROM: Darcy McFee
SUBJECT: Re: Re: Next Meeting
DATE: July 17th

I am traveling now and will not be answering e-mails until I return on July 21st.

Thanks!

Darcy

TO: PAWS Listserv
FROM: Sam Fulgram, Jr.
SUBJECT: Re: Re: Re: Next Meeting
DATE: July 17th

Whoa boy! Do you realize you just sent out your love note to the entire Poetry Association of the Western Suburbs listserv?

Cheers,

Sam

P.S.—That mole? You've got my imagination running wild. As long as the entire organization knows about it now, would you mind divulging its location? I'd sleep better at night knowing it.

TO: PAWS Listserv
FROM: Betsy Midchester
SUBJECT: Re: Re: Re: Re: Next Meeting
DATE: July 17th

Hi all,

Well! That last message from "Mikey" Stroud certainly made my day. I thought at first the message was addressed to me. As I had no memory of placing my foot in Mike's crotch, I naturally assumed that I needed an adjustment of my medication so that I wouldn't forget such episodes in the future. Now I see it's simply Michael ("Down Boy") Stroud and our esteemed Secretary of the Galloping Mont Blaaaaanc who need the medication adjustments. Thanks, in any case, for a much-needed lift in an otherwise humdrum day.

Betsy Midchester
Treasurer/PAWS

TO: PAWS Listserv
FROM: Lisa Drago-Harse
SUBJECT: Re: Re: Re: Re: Re: Next Meeting
DATE: July 17th

This is a nightmare. I'm not quite sure what to say except that life is unpredictable and often irreversible. While I do not wish to go into details or make excuses for the above e-mail from Michael Stroud, I would like to clarify one thing: that was not my foot in your crotch, Michael. But your belief that it was my foot in your crotch explains a few things concerning your subsequent behavior toward me that were up until this moment a mystery.

LDH

TO: PAWS Listserv
FROM: Michael Stroud
SUBJECT: Re: Re: Re: Re: Re: Re: Next Meeting
DATE: July 17th

I'm

TO: PAWS Listserv
FROM: Michael Stroud
SUBJECT: Re: Re: Re: Re: Re: Re: Re: Next Meeting
DATE: July 17th

I hit the send button by mistake before I was ready. This isn't my day, to say the least! I'm sorry!!!! I'd like to apologize to the entire PAWS community, and also to Lisa's husband Richard and to Darcy. And to you, Lisa. I don't mean to make excuses for myself, but I would like to say that I've been under a tremendous amount of pressure of late, at school, at home, and I am nothing if not vulnerable and flawed. All I can say is that in poetry I find some solace for the petty actions of others and the sometimes monstrous actions of which I'm all too capable. As déclassé as Truth and Beauty are these days, it is in such expressions as those of Matthew Arnold, Keats, Byron, and Shelley that I look for my meager draught of the Divine. And sometimes, I must admit, I seek in the affection of my fellow poetry lovers, the divinity which I myself lack. I ask you all to blame me, not Lisa, for what has happened.

But if not your foot, Lisa, then whose?
Michael Stroud

TO: PAWS Listserv
FROM: Greg Rudolfsky
SUBJECT: Re: Re: Re: Re: Re: Re: Re: Re: RESPECT
DATE: July 17th

Just a little bit, Just a little bit.
Sock it to me, sock it to me, sock it to me, sock it to me, sock it to
me, sock it to me, sock it to me, sock it to me, RESPECT, Just a
little bit, just a little bit . . .

TO: PAWS Listserv
FROM: Samantha M. Poulsen, RN
SUBJECT: Fecund Poets
DATE: July 17th

I do not care whose foot is in whose crotch, but I think it's insulting and idiotic that so-called educated people would use such
phrases as, "the fecund wetness bursting with your being and
effulgence." And officers of the PAWS at that!

TO: PAWS Listserv
FROM: Richard Drago-Harse
SUBJECT: Re: Fecund Poets
DATE: July 17th

I would like to tender my resignation from the Poets of the Western Suburbs, as I will be tendering my resignation from several
other areas of my life. I only belonged to PAWS in any case be-

cause of my wife's interest in poetry. I wanted to share her interests, but clearly not all of them.

TO: PAWS listserv:
FROM: Darcy McFee
SUBJECT: Re: Re: Fecund Poets
DATE: July 22nd

Well, it seems that our little organization has been busy in my absence. I have over 300 new messages in my e-mail account, all, it seems from my fellow poetry lovers! I haven't yet had a chance to read your exchanges, but I will soon. In the meantime, I wanted to convey some exciting news. This weekend, while attending a workshop at Wright State in Dayton, I ran into the former Poet Laureate, Billy Collins, who has agreed to be our special guest at our annual Poetry Bash in Oak Park. He said he's heard quite a lot about our organization in recent days and that our board had achieved near legendary status in the poetry community. I knew this would make you as proud as it makes me.

TO: PAWS listserv
FROM: Darcy McFee
SUBJECT: Twee
DATE: July 24th

So this is how it is. Upon reading the 300 e-mails that collected in my inbox over the weekend, my mind is a riot of emotions. I have not slept for nearly forty-eight hours. Never before have I been so insulted. Yet, I also know that I am, at least in part, to blame. Had I not stuck my foot in Michael Stroud's crotch, none of this would have happened. Twitching like a slug that's had salt poured on it? That hurts, Michael. It really does. I didn't realize you were so shallow. But in reading your collective e-mails, I see that at least half our membership has a decidedly sadistic bent. In any case, it was not your crotch I aimed for, Michael, but the crotch of our Vice President, Amir Bathshiri, with whom I have long been intimately acquainted, both of us having lost our spouses several years ago. If the seating arrangements in the Sir Francis Drake Room were any less cramped, none of these misunderstandings would have occurred. Of course I never would have tried to fondle you, Michael. In the first place, you are the most boring, tedious person I have met in my life, and believe me, as Chair of the English Dept. at Roosevelt, I have met my share of boring, tedious people. You recite poetry with all the grace of a highway sign that cautions one to beware of falling rocks. But enough! I know that it is my errant foot to blame. Amir and I have talked this over and have decided to withdraw from PAWS as well as from academia. Early retirement calls, Michael and Lisa, and I will give neither of you a thought as I walk along the beach hand-in-hand with Amir in the months and years to come, listening to the mermaids singing each to each.

Yes, Michael, I find you and your crotch and your paramour the very essence of Twee.

TO: PAWS Listserv
FROM: Betsy Midchester/Treasurer
SUBJECT: New Elections
DATE: July 30th

Please note that the agenda for our next meeting has changed. We will spend most of the meeting on new elections to be held for the positions of President, Vice President, and Secretary of our organization. Note, too, that we will no longer be meeting in the Sir Francis Drake Room of the Bensenville Hampton Inn. Instead, we will be meeting in the cafeteria of the Enchanted Gardens Residence for Seniors in Glen Ellyn. The change in venue was planned well in advance of recent events, so members should not read anything into this (though if any organization's members are skilled at reading between the lines, it should be ours). Please think about whom you would like to nominate for these important positions in our organization. And in the meantime, please remember to always be conscious and considerate of your audience.

Peace and poetry,
Betsy Midchester
Treasurer and Acting President/PAWS

ROBIN HEMLEY is the author of eight books of nonfiction and fiction and the winner of many awards including a 2008 Guggenheim Fellowship, the Nelson Algren Award for Short Fiction from the *Chicago Tribune,* the *Story* magazine Humor Prize, an Independent Press Book Award, two Pushcart Prizes, and many others. His fiction, nonfiction, and poetry have been published in the United States, Great Britain, Germany, Japan, the Philippines, Hong Kong, and elsewhere, and he frequently teaches creative writing workshops around the world. He has been widely anthologized and has published his work in such periodicals as the *New York Times*, *Orion*, the *Wall Street Journal*, the *Chicago Tribune*, *New York* magazine, and many of the finest literary magazines in the United States. He is a Senior Editor of the *Iowa Review* as well as the editor of a popular online journal, *Defunct* (Defunctmag.com). He currently directs the Nonfiction Writing Program at the University of Iowa and is the founder and organizer of NonfictioNow, a biennial conference that explores nonfiction in its myriad forms.